MASTERSON MADE

MASTERSON SERIES BOOK FOUR

LISA LANG BLAKENEY

WRITERGIRL PRESS

LICENSE NOTE

This book contains mature content, including graphic sex. Please do not continue reading if you are under the age of 18 or if this type of content is disturbing to you.

To Mommy

BOOK LIST

The Masterson Series

Masterson

Masterson Unleashed

Masterson In Love

Masterson Made

Joseph Loves Juliette

The King Brothers Series

Claimed

Indebted

Broken

Promised

The Nighthawk Series

Gunslinger

Wolf

Diesel

The Valencia Mafia Series

Coming Soon. Get Notified!

INTRODUCTION

Now that my heart belongs to Elizabeth, I need to make sure she doesn't crush it. Now that I'm committed to giving her everything, I need to ensure that I'm left with nothing. Now that I've gotten everything I ever wanted, I need to make certain that things don't fall apart...and I will fight like hell for it.

The first night the dark and dangerous Roman Masterson laid eyes on Elizabeth, the earth shifted beneath him, changing the trajectory of his life forever.

The only thing that existed for him from that

moment on was her, but nobody said a happily-ever-after was going to be easy, especially when one gunshot could change everything.

PROLOGUE

ROMAN

It amazes me how time can become an abstract construct when some of your senses are muted and others heightened. I am seated on a cold concrete floor and there is a large blindfold made of a sour-smelling fabric wrapped tightly around my skull, completely blinding me to my surroundings.

There is an irritatingly loud song playing on a loop in a language I don't understand. Based on some phonetics of the song, my guess is it's a Russian band. My hands are tied tightly behind my back with what feels like two zip ties, my ankles are duct taped together, and I have no idea how long I've been here. My guess is five hours, but it could easily have been fifteen minutes. Who the hell knows.

I'm fuming.

It's been a long time since anyone's gotten one up on me, which is why I'm furious with myself that I've allowed this to happen. The old man is right. I must be slipping. I'm getting entirely too soft and complacent. This is my fault.

When I was a kid, I was always the tallest and the strongest boy in the neighborhood and no one could beat me. As I grew into an adult, my reputation preceded me, and I didn't have to be the biggest or the strongest because I was the most feared. Now, I find myself in a unique position. The men in this room either don't fear me or don't know that they should.

I've long since stopped struggling to free myself from the ties that bind my wrists and ankles, because I need to think clearly and reserve my energy. My sole mission at this point is to get back to Elizabeth and my baby boy. That's it.

All I see are their faces behind this mask. All I hear is the sound of their laughter. All I smell is the warm jasmine on her skin and the faint baby soft scent of his. So I need to be really confident about any action I take next to get out of this clusterfuck.

I can't let them down.

Not again.

I hear a heavy door creak open and then foot-steps. Based on my count, there are at least two men crossing the room toward me. They speak to each other in brief terse sentences in what I'm now posi-tive is the Russian language, and while I don't under-stand what they're saying, I can sense things from their tone.

They're worried.

And they should be.

Once Camden, Cutter, Stone, or Joseph find out what happened to me there will be some slow singing and flower bringing for these jackasses. They've kidnapped the wrong motherfucker and there will be a reckoning.

"Wake up," one man orders as he pushes the makeshift scarf off of my eyes.

I slowly raise my head and open my eyes. The lighting in the room is dim, which fortunately helps my pupils adjust faster than if it was normally lit. I'm being held in an area which is larger than I thought. It looks like an unused storage facility with unfin-ished concrete floors and walls. The only thing inside here besides me is a battered-looking utility sink, a portable boom box which was no doubt the source of the wretched Russian rock music, and some sealed cardboard boxes on the other side of the room.

I make sure to stare my captors directly in the eyes. Just by their body language, I can tell who the one in charge probably is—the one who's silent. The one asking all the questions is probably the enforcer, the man who puts in the work so that the boss can sit and analyze my responses. How I answer determines whether I live or die.

"What business you have with Patricia?" he asks in broken English with a thick Russian accent.

I've been hired to handle a lot of jobs over my career as a professional fixer, and I've never been under any delusion that my past couldn't come back to haunt me. In fact, I've lived my life knowing that it could. So the King Brothers and I pay an exorbitant amount of money to a private detective to keep tabs on all of our clients and most of our enemies. We usually stay on top of most everyone, but I didn't see this one coming.

That's because Patricia wasn't a client.

She was a favor.

"None."

The asshole kicks me swiftly in the ribs with his steel-toed boot.

"Wrong answer. What business you have with Patricia?" he repeats.

"*Nichego*," I say in a truculent manner.

It just so happens that I know about five words in Russian. I learned them from a female bartender who worked for the club years ago when my father first bought it. One of them was her safe word, *nichego*, which means nothing in English.

The enforcer's eyes widen when he hears me say the word. The other man doesn't express any emotion at all, but I know that I've at least created some doubt. They aren't sure who I am and what I know. They might even question whether it's possible that I understand Russian since I know such a random word. All of this uncertainty is buying me time. I need it so that my boys can find me. If I know Camden, he probably has trackers on shit I don't even know about. If anyone can find me, he will.

I hear the rusty hinges of the door creak again before I see it open. Another person enters the room and both men immediately straighten their spines and stop speaking. Now I realize that they must both be enforcers because this woman strolls in the room like she is the real boss.

She looks like a middle-aged Nikita on a budget.

Her cheap high heels clack against the solid floor and her hips swish exaggeratedly. She's dressed in a long, leopard print, slip dress and a pair of very high black pumps. Her puffed-up lips are painted a deep, crimson red, no doubt to distract us from the fact that her face has been pulled so tightly that she resembles a sixty-year-old Bratz doll.

She stands in front of me and gives me a pensive long look. I stare back at her just as intently. Something about me intrigues her because the corner of her painted lips lifts in a small smirk.

"Do you speak Russian?"

"Nyet," I answer with the second word I know, but this is easy. Many people know how to say no in Russian just by watching television, but again the point here is to create doubt, not certainty.

The woman beams this time.

"You lie to me?"

"Nyet," I repeat.

She walks in a circle around me and the squeak of her heels grows increasingly more annoying than the god-awful music they were playing earlier.

"The beautiful boy you put your hands on at Drexel Village is my son."

At least she gets right to the point.

"Your son needs some manners," I tell her, as I

contemplate how the hell this woman knows who I am and where she could find me.

"Who are you to speak of manners when you have no respect?"

This conversation is actually helpful. The woman only has a slight hint of a Russian accent which tells me she's probably American born and was perhaps raised in a Russian neighborhood but not one in Philadelphia or else I'd know her. The mention of the word respect also reveals to me she's indeed Bratva. Mafia types are obsessed with being paid respect. The question about her now is from which family and where.

"I don't respect any man who harasses a woman just because he can," I tell her.

"Is this what Patricia told you? That my son harassed her?"

"She didn't have to tell me anything. It was obvious what your son was doing."

"Based on what evidence?"

"He broke into her apartment and searched through her things like a pervert. He placed spyware on her computer, which is illegal. He followed her to her car on numerous occasions, asking her out after she already turned him down. That is stalking. You need more? I could go on."

The woman points two of her fingers to the ground as some sort of signal. The enforcer whom I'm growing to loathe at this point kicks me two times in the same spot with that damn metal tipped boot of his. She's got these dogs of hers trained well. I need not hear a snap to know that he's successfully broken one of my ribs this time. The pain comes swiftly as I struggle to breathe.

"Your information is incorrect. My son doesn't need to stalk some *shlyukha* who can't pay her rent on time. You made a mistake."

I know for a fact that my intel is correct. Cam found the spyware, Cutter found his prints on her underwear drawer, and I had Stone watch the woman for a week. This woman's sociopathic son was approaching Patricia damn near every day. He was obsessed with her, and anyone with an ounce of common sense could see that his fascination with the girl was going to go south soon.

"My intel is solid," I say through pained breaths.

"You put your hands on the wrong man."

"And he was stalking the wrong woman."

The woman's face tightens further, as if that's even possible. It's so full of Botox she has a permanent scowl on her face already.

"Are you a cop?"

"Nyet."

Her eyelid jumps every time I try replying in my terrible Russian. That must be one of her pet peeves, as I'm no doubt butchering the pronunciations.

"Then who hired you or who is Patricia to you?"

This is the second time they have asked me this specific question which makes me think Patricia is seriously hurt or they plan to hurt her because they're trying to calculate what the ramifications might be afterward.

"She's no one to me."

The woman waves her hand twice to the quieter goon and he hands her a gun. She points the modified Springfield Hellcat at me with focused intent. This woman is dead-ass serious, she hasn't come to play.

"I am not in the habit of torture or long conversations. You are either useful to me or you aren't. As far as I can tell you're just muscle for someone else. I want the person who hired you and maybe you'll live, but if you're not willing to share that information, there are other ways I can get it. Ways that don't involve you still breathing."

I've learned over the years that women in power are often more calculated and much more ruthless than men. On top of all of that, they take shit personally. Did I break her son's arm? Yes, but only in self-defense. That asswipe tried to sneak a punch so he deserved it.

I say nothing more in response to my captor's threat because there is nothing left to say. At this point, I need to think about how I'm going to buy myself some more time until the Kings get here. Elizabeth must be out of her mind, worried about me.

"Give me his wallet and his phone," she commands them.

Dammit, I forgot about that. When they tased me at my car, they caught me completely off guard. I own two wallets and two phones. One set contains my official identification and the other is a burner phone and fake ID for work. I usually keep my genuine stuff in my glove compartment and not on me, but I didn't have time to switch them out after leaving the store, so now these assholes have my actual information.

"So... we have a license with an address. A prestigious address. Right around the corner from where my friends picked you up. Interesting. You're not only good-looking but you must make good money as well, Roman Masterson. Very impressive for someone your age."

This is going to shit really quickly. What is taking those fuckers so long to find me?

"His phone is unlocked," the boot kicker offers excitedly.

"Not very smart, Mr. Masterson. I see you have a picture of the wife and kid on the home screen. How quaint. She's not what I was expecting, though. A man like you could do a lot better."

This walking piece of plastic is dead when I get out of these restraints.

"Fuck you."

Her eyes deaden after the insult.

"You're sensitive about the family, huh? Well, I totally understand that because guess what? I'm the same way."

Within seconds she lifts her arm, points and shoots with pinpoint accuracy at my right shoulder. It's as if I'm watching in slow motion as the bullet releases from the chamber and plunges into my flesh through what feels like bone. Since they bound my hands behind my back, all I can do is bend over and grimace from the intense pain as blood oozes from the wound and trickles down my arm.

I can't believe the bitch actually shot me.

1

ROMAN
Six Weeks Earlier

Two of the most important people in my life are fast asleep on their sides in the middle of the bed. One is snoring louder than a truck driver, but for me no woman has ever looked sexier. The other has his mouth slightly parted, drunk off of his mother's breastmilk, and no baby in this world has ever looked more angelic.

I pull out my cell phone and snap a picture for posterity. I want to always remember the two loves of my life just like this—unfiltered and unbothered by the world. Afterward, I gently scoop my boy in my arms and take him to the nursery so they both can have a little uninterrupted rest.

Although falling asleep is a pretty common thing after Elizabeth nurses our rambunctious eight-month-son, Knox, I know that part of the reason she is dead to the world is that she is completely exhausted. No matter how much I try to help with Knox, I am no substitute for him wanting his mother's tit. He is wiping her out in a way that I never could.

I've been encouraging her for three weeks now to finally wean my boy off of her breastmilk, but as usual I've been outvoted. Elizabeth wants him to receive all the nutritional benefits from breastmilk for at least a year, and just like a Masterson man, my son is taking full advantage of a good thing.

But something has to give.

It wasn't that long ago that Elizabeth was bruised and battered in a horrific accident when she was pregnant with Knox that damn near took a year off of my life; yet she feeds him every couple of hours, plays many development games with him, does a full day's work, and if she has a smidgeon of energy left, she may take pity on me and give me a lazy fuck.

But that's the thing.

She rarely has any energy left after a day of being

a wonderful mother and a responsible business owner, so lazy fucks are far and few between. Needless to say, something's going to have to change soon, because I need to be inside of Elizabeth like I need oxygen to breathe.

A weird sounding chime goes off from the smart device on the nightstand. Even our dog, Mr. Tibbs, raises and tilts his head in question of the odd ring. I suspect it's some sort of alarm Elizabeth has set to wake herself up from her impromptu nap.

I try turning it off quickly, but it's too late as she reluctantly stirs from her sleep. I brush a finger down the side of her face, adjusting some stray curls behind her ear.

"Why don't you sleep another twenty," I whisper.

"I can't," she responds groggily. "I shouldn't even be asleep now."

"Why?"

She notices Knox is missing from the bed.

"The baby!"

"I put him in the crib. Don't worry, I've got him today."

"My meeting—"

"What meeting? It's Saturday, Duchess."

She must be delirious with sleep. Her days seem to be seamlessly blending into each other.

"It was the only day he could talk."

She tries inching the sheet and quilt down with her feet to wake herself up. The central air is on high and keeps our room cool enough for her to sleep under layers. I yank them back up to her neck. Pissed that she's actually attempting to work on a Saturday when she hasn't had a good night's sleep in months.

"*He* who?"

"The new president of Cabot University. He's considering working exclusively with us. He would promote the use of the app through official university communications, potentially exposing us to thousands of students."

"Where's Cabot University?"

"It's a small school upstate, but they're connected to the University of Pennsylvania network."

"That's big news, baby. I can't believe you're just telling me about it."

"I didn't want to jinx it."

"You know I don't believe in all of that superstitious BS."

"Yeah, but I've been let down so many times before from deals that almost happened. I just wanted to wait to tell you until I was at least close to securing the deal."

I sit on the edge of our bed and slide my hand underneath the covers near the apex of Elizabeth's thighs.

"If you would just let me help you secure a few paid clients, you would never need to feel disappointed again. In fact, helping you would be my pleasure."

The heat emanating from my fiancée's crotch as I knead the inside of her thigh makes me feel stiff in my own. I want inside of my woman in the worst way.

"It won't mean the same if you just buy me business relationships, Roman."

Elizabeth abruptly rolls over toward the nightstand and reaches for her cell phone once she hears it ding, immediately ending the physical contact between my hand and her thigh.

Now I'm just fucking annoyed.

"Why won't it mean the same? Do you actually believe that all the millionaires in this country earn their money with hard work and honest deals?" I scoff.

"I don't need to be a millionaire like *some* people. I just want to help students find scholarships for college and make a decent living while I do it."

Elizabeth picks up her phone and starts scrolling

through her text messages as if this conversation is boring her. It's been a minute since I tied her pretty ass up to the headboard and fucked her sideways. I think she's overdue.

"You know what I mean, Elizabeth, and put the phone down."

"I'm sending my friend Patty some money. Wait, a second."

I can't help but notice the confirmation screen on her phone and it surprises me. She just sent this Patty person a thousand dollars and even though we live comfortably, that's still a lot of money to just give someone, especially a woman I've never heard of.

"Who's Patty?"

"An old friend from school. Her creepy landlord is giving her some problems so the money will help her pay the security deposit for a new place. Maybe you can go down there and talk to him until she finds something else?"

Lately, my Duchess worries about everything and everyone besides the one thing she should be, herself.

"Are you finished?" I ask impatiently because I'm sick and tired of competing with every device in this house.

She places the phone on her lap and slowly rolls

her head up to glare at me. This woman I adore has developed a serious attitude problem which I attribute to a sleep deprivation and a lack of some good dick in her life.

"Fine, you want to talk about my business? Well, I think it's perfectly okay for us to have different approaches toward how we accomplish our goals. You have your way of doing things and I have mine."

"Yeah, but it's my approach that actually works."

"You're so arrogant."

"Is it I'm arrogant or that I'm right?"

"It sounds like you're throwing up in my face you pay all the bills around here?"

Damn, she must be sleep deprived. I totally wasn't saying that shit.

"No, Duchess, not at all. I'm just saying that all the strategies I've learned over the years like buying favors, arranging backdoor deals, and leveraging influence over people to get what I need is what works."

"I think you're comparing oranges to apples. The two of us are in very different lines of work, and that's not the way I'm going to build School Bucks into a brand that every college student in the world can use. I'm going to do it my way. No skipping the line."

I grunt to myself, which is the equivalent of me rolling my eyes. While I've never attended an ivy league university like Elizabeth and her friends, I've learned everything I need to know on the streets, specifically under the tutelage of my father, Joseph. One thing he's always impressed upon me is that nobody gets brownie points for doing shit the hard way.

Unfortunately, Elizabeth and I have had this conversation more times than I can count and it always ends up the same way. Me pissed that she won't permit me to help her grow her business in the way that I know how and her apologizing for making me angry by wrapping her pretty lips around my dick. That is definitely the easiest solution to shutting me up, but sadly that's not the way this conversation is going to end because Knox just started waking from his nap. I can hear the echo of his raspy baby babble through the five gazillion monitors Elizabeth has placed all over the damn house.

"Ah, there he is," she says, sounding almost relieved that she has an excuse to end our conversation.

When she rises from the bed, I place my palm firmly against her chest, getting a quick feel of her right tit for good measure. Her nipple pebbles from my brief touch and a petty part of me dies inside. Elizabeth's breasts are round and full from breast-feeding and look amazing, it's a fucking shame neither one of them have been in my mouth for days.

"I said I've got him."

"Okay," she reluctantly agrees.

When I enter the nursery, my little bruiser is on his feet, hands wrapped around the railing, with a huge grin on his face. I can't help but give him one in return. He has his mother's smile and my deep-set eyes. Other than Elizabeth, I don't think I've ever loved anyone or anything more in my life. You can't help but adore this little bundle of baby brute force. He's already got the great makings of a Masterson man—he's irresistible and unstoppable. Nobody can say no to him.

"Hey, little monster, why aren't you letting Mommy get any rest? You know you're cock blocking me big time, right?"

I grin as Knox raises his arms and babbles something totally incoherent that only his mother ever seems to understand.

"Roman!" Elizabeth hollers from our bedroom.

"Watch your mouth. Don't curse in front of the baby."

Knox giggles as if he understands every word I've just said and his mother's response. Hell, maybe he does. I wouldn't put it past Elizabeth to have given birth to a genius.

"Relax, nerd," I say, practically laughing myself. "Go back to sleep or something."

"He's probably hungry."

"How can you be hungry, dude?" I ask him in a small voice. "You just drank from my favorite tit."

He babbles a string of nonsense words together with the most stern look across his face. I'm pretty sure this little boy just cursed me out. I pick him up and sniff his butt. Great, I smell nothing putrid. I slide my finger inside of the diaper to feel if he's wet (he's not)—perfect. So the only thing left to do now is feed him *again* like his mother suggested, although I'm not sure where he's putting all of it.

"You must have one hell of a metabolism," I whisper in his ear as he babbles with great inflection.

"Is that so?" I say in response, chuckling to myself. I don't have a clue what he's talking about, but it's definitely something.

I dip my head back into our bedroom. "Is there a bottle in the fridge?"

"Yes, but—"

"Then we're good."

"But I—"

"Duchess, I don't care if you go back to sleep or get ready for your call, but I've got this. Give Mommy a kiss, little monster."

I walk back over to Elizabeth and lean in with Knox tucked under my arm like a football. She gives him a sleepy kiss on his mouth.

"Love you, peanut."

Turns out that allowing him within a few feet of his mother was a bad idea because our new little master manipulator cries as soon as I pull him away.

"Give him here," she commands.

Elizabeth holds her arms out for me to hand him over.

"No."

2

ROMAN

"Just give him here, Roman." She makes the "gimme" sign with her hands. "Aww, peanut, don't cry. Maybe I should just nurse him instead."

I see the tears of mama guilt swell in Elizabeth's eyes.

This shit has got to stop.

"Duchess, babies cry, especially this one. It's what they do. He'll stop once I give him the bottle."

"I don't think it's just that he's hungry. He misses me. I bet it's because I don't spend enough time with him."

With *him*? Shit, she doesn't spend enough time with me, but this isn't the time for that conversation.

"I am familiar with having a shitty mother and you are not that. You are a fantastic mom who runs her own business, which means you're busy, not negligent. We will figure it out and Knox will be fine. He's got the both of us."

I rub my hand down the front of Knox's face to wipe the tears and snot away and he giggles. I think Elizabeth and I have made the happiest or craziest boy on the planet. He flips from crying to laughing in a fraction of a second.

"See, he's fine."

Elizabeth smiles and I feel her sense of relief deep in my chest. It's my job to protect her in every way, physically and emotionally, so when I've done my job right I feel a sense of accomplishment. Sometimes I think the responsibility of taking care of her and Knox are the only two reasons I get up in the morning; like they're the only two things that stop me from becoming my baser self and breaking a man's neck when somebody inevitably pisses me off. They are my life and keep me grounded and motivated. Everything I do now, I do for them.

"So what have you decided to do, beautiful?" I ask her.

"I know it's a Saturday, but I'm going to take the call."

"So go brush your teeth, take a shower, then handle your call. Me and the little monster are going to have a long conversation about how Cookie Monster handled Elmo like a boss in the last episode we watched."

"What are you talking about, crazy man?"

"It was a good character building episode. Cookie Monster is the only Muppet that is always sure of what he wants. A monster after my own heart. He wants cookies and that's it. If you're not talking shit about cookies, then he isn't interested."

Elizabeth lets out a laugh at my commentary, a genuine laugh, and my dick damn near gets hard as a rock as I watch her full tits bounce in her tiny, white tank top. It's been forever since I've been able to make love to my girl the way she really likes it—hard and nasty. That's because there are a myriad of time constraints, two leaky breasts, and one crying baby that gets in the way all the damn time.

I try to remember my stepmother's words at times like this, "this too shall pass" but right now Juliette's words don't hold any comfort for me. All I can hear is the annoying voice in my head whenever I take a whiff of Elizabeth, much less look at her.

You need that pussy, but you ain't getting some today.

"Only you could make that analogy of a beloved childhood character."

I think Elizabeth just said something, but I don't even know what it was because I'm staring at her tits and ass with nefarious intent. Her eyebrows raise once she notices what's up.

"Uh-uh, Roman, I've got to shower and your baby is hungry," she says with a warning.

"You mean *the baby* who's happily playing with my ears right now? The baby who couldn't care less about a bottle of milk?"

Knox has some sort of fascination with ears and earrings. Elizabeth can never wear any dangling earrings around him because before you can blink, he's already tossed one of them clear across the room. On top of being good-natured, good-looking, and smart, my son also seems to be athletically inclined. I see a major baseball or football career in his future.

"Roman."

"Baby, why don't I put him in the playpen with a bottle of your gently warmed breastmilk and come take a shower with you."

"I would love that but my call is in twenty

minutes and nothing that the two of us ever starts finishes in twenty minutes. Plus, it's not a good idea to leave him alone with his bottle. He's too young. What if he chokes?"

"I don't think this boy has ever wasted one droplet of your milk. He definitely will not choke on it."

She turns her lips up at me like I'm being a bad parent.

Hmm, maybe I am.

"Okay, fine," I bargain. "You know I'm not all about the quickies, but how about I take care of you in under ten minutes? Knox can stay in the room. Problem solved."

"Roman!"

"What? We did it before."

"He was six-weeks-old then. He didn't know what we were doing."

"And you think he knows what we're doing now?" I ask incredulously.

"No," she says emphatically. "We're not doing it."

"I'm not asking permission, Duchess."

My voice drops an octave, and Elizabeth's eyes widen. It's been a long time since I've made any overt sexual demands of her because we've been overwhelmed with our new lives and our new baby, but just when I notice a flicker of desire rise in her eyes, our little puppet master lets out the loudest wail.

"Whaaaaa!"

And then he gives the side of my face a firm whack.

I never thought I would think this about my own flesh and blood, but Knox Masterson truly is a cock blocker, and now that I think about it he's been that way since the very beginning.

Elizabeth went into labor as I was hitting that swollen, pregnant pussy of hers from the back. Those were good times. She was always horny, and I was a willing participant to satisfy her every need. I was stroking her very carefully, making sure not to cause Knox or her any discomfort, but I also was talking major shit to her that night. Real dirty. She was sopping wet way before I even slipped inside of her. She came twice before I even got a good rhythm going, and I was literally mid-stroke when the contractions began.

At first I panicked, thinking she was contracting because I had gone too deep, but no, it was just Knox making a grand entrance. He was letting me know to get out of the way because he was coming into the world... and I would not be *coming* at all that night.

The more things change, the more they stay the same.

"See? I knew it. He's hungry."

"All right, boy. Let's go get this milk you love so much and watch a little *Sesame Street*. I'll play with Mommy another time."

Elizabeth stands up and gives me a quick peck on the lips.

"Thank you, honey. I can always shower again tonight," she says with a mischievous grin.

That one statement soothes the selfish part of me for now.

Of course she's right.

There's always tonight once this little hell raiser goes to sleep.

Or maybe the next.

3

ELIZABETH

When I was pregnant with Knox, I wouldn't say that my life changed significantly. On the contrary, many things stayed wonderfully the same. I continued to work, periodically hung out with Sloan, but spent most of my time with Roman playing house and getting ready for our son's arrival. It was a beautiful and exciting time in our lives. My body was healing nicely from the horrible accident I had been in, Roman and I were madly in love with each other and also with this new human being who we hadn't even met yet, but something shifted once I gave birth.

It was easy to become immersed in nothing but Roman when it was just the two and a half of us. The energy of his expansive body and hard edges fills a room the minute he walks inside and I ravenously fed off of it, but now there is another force competing for his attention and my time. That energy force is better known as Knox Masterson.

The new love of my life.

When I stare into my son's eyes I can see all the hopes and dreams that I want for him: independence, self-determination, romantic love, and world frackin' peace. It's a tall order, but I want him to have everything in life he'll ever desire, and I know that begins with having parents who are just as happy apart as they are together.

For me, that individual happiness means putting off our wedding while I take a moment to concentrate on being the best mother I can be and making a success of my business, School Bucks. The difficulty with achieving my personal aim has been how to balance these parts of my life that I love, need, and desperately want.

Let's take hygiene, for example. It's been a very long time since I've showered, put on makeup, and gotten dressed in something other than a tank top and shorts. I spend most of my time taking care of Knox or working on the code for my app. I rarely have time for much else, but tonight I promised my friend Zoe that I'd attend her thirtieth birthday party so soap and a little lip gloss are mandatory.

Zoe is a super talented tattoo artist who illustrated my Masterson Made ink and someone who has since become a good friend. While our backgrounds are very different, she is a thirty-year-old bisexual who grew up in foster care and reads people's palms for fun, and I am a twenty-five-year-old heterosexual computer nerd who grew up in a two-parent household in the suburbs, I find that in most of the important ways we think alike.

While I definitely want to be a part of celebrating this milestone birthday for her, this is the first time that I am leaving Knox to just go hang out. I mean it's one thing to leave him with Roman to go grocery shopping or when I have a meeting with one of my coders, but to go out for a night with the girls to party? That's something entirely different, and in some ways I feel guilty about it. I feel like my mother was home for every single day of my life. That's what good mothers do, right?

"Hey, baby."

"Hey."

"You all right?"

I'm working hair gel quickly through some of my curls to tame the flyaways and frizz. Sometimes this whole curly girl thing is hard work.

"Yeah."

"The Glamazon is at the door."

"I thought you were going to stop calling her that."

"I only say it in front of you."

I don't hear any movement downstairs.

"Well, did you let her in?"

"Did you want me to?"

I shake my head at him.

"You're a piece of work, Roman."

"Is she going to Zoe's with you?" He snickers as I head downstairs to the door.

"Yeah, she's driving."

I open the front door to greet my friend and as usual she looks like a million bucks dressed in a sleek gold dress with strappy gold heels to match. Now I'm worried that I'm going to be seriously underdressed for this party.

Sloan greets me with her arm raised and a bottle of champagne in her hand. "All the girls in the club gettin' tipsy!" She sings the lyrics to a familiar rap song as she enters the house.

Roman isn't impressed.

"Sloan."

"Roman."

Their greetings for each other are curt, but at least they're respectful.

"Elizabeth said you'll be driving tonight?"

His question is more rhetorical than anything. I'm sure he's commenting more about the fact that she's the designated driver but has arrived at our front door with a bottle in her hand.

"That's right. The bottle is for Zoe."

She runs over in her heels and gives me a hug.

"You look amazing, Bitsy. Look at my little stay-at-home mom all cleaned up."

"Whatever, girl." I smile, slightly embarrassed by her compliment. It only affirms the fact that I've probably looked like a disaster for months.

"Where's that big ol' baby of yours?"

"He's napping."

"Damn, why don't I ever get to see him when he's awake?"

"Because you never come over here at a reasonable hour," Roman interjects.

Sloan rolls her eyes and continues talking to me.

"You want a drink before we go? You know, to

kind of loosen up all your rusty parts and get ready for tonight's shenanigans?"

"What the fuck, Sloan?" Roman asks incredulously.

"I meant that the drinks will lube up her rusty parts for *dancing*. What do you think I'm talking about?" Sloan gives him the side-eye. "Relax."

"This is not a conversation I'm trying to have or hear."

"Good, it wasn't meant for your sensitive ears anyhow."

Roman looks at me, and I give him a stilted smile. It's clear that he is trying his level best to be on his best behavior and Sloan is just being Sloan. He knows better than anyone that I've been looking forward to the prospect of going out for a little baby-free fun, and he doesn't want to ruin it for me. I just wish the two of them wouldn't antagonize each other so much. I'm already on edge about leaving Knox tonight.

"Let me get my heels and we can go, Sloan. I'll be right back."

"Wear the fuck 'em heels. You know, the nude colored ones with the crisscross straps. Those will look great with the jeans."

I can hear Roman growling from here.

"I'm wearing the wedges," I tell her.

"Borrrrinnngggg."

I take a second to pop in on Knox to make sure the temperature in his room is comfortable and that he's sleeping soundly.

He looks like an angel.

He's flat on his back with his arms spread high above his head and his head tilted to the side. His eyelashes are long and flutter slightly when I graze my finger down the side of his face.

"I love you," I whisper. "I'll be home soon."

I can't explain the feeling in my stomach as I grab my shoes and my handbag. I'm excited to spend the evening out and have a little mindless fun, but I don't feel entirely good about it either.

When I return to the living room, Sloan is searching for another bottle in our bar and Roman is sitting on his favorite chaise lounge, legs spread, and arms crossed in front of his chest, quietly watching. He's annoyed, but I'm not surprised. I love her, but Sloan has that effect on many people.

"What are you looking for?" I ask her.

"Shots! Shots! Shot, shot, shot, shots!" she replies with a chant we used to say on our way bar hopping in college.

Roman rolls his eyes with disapproval. "Would

you quiet down? My son is asleep and you're agitating Mr. Tibbs."

Sloan bends down to scratch our dog's tummy. He's flat on his back with his legs spread wide like he hasn't a care in the world.

"Oh yeah, he's really agitated," Sloan mocks.

"You want tequila, right?" I point to the bottle of Silver Patron. "It's right in front of you."

"No, we should drink the expensive stuff. I know the dark knight of yours is holding out on the grand tequila. Where do you keep the good shit, Roman?"

"The good shit is for special occasions," he answers flatly.

"But this is a special occasion. It's Zoe's birthday."

"That's not a special occasion for me."

"You can be so selfish sometimes. Zoe is your baby mama's friend, so that makes it a special occasion."

"Still not special."

"Ugh, I just want to have a shot with Bitsy before we go. This is just as much a celebration for her as it is for Zoe. It's the first time you've let her out of her gilded cage since my gorgeous godson was born. That's something to celebrate."

Roman raises his eyebrows in reaction to Sloan's

comment, although I'm not sure which part of it he takes more issue with. On one hand, for whatever reason, Sloan has convinced herself and probably our immediate circle of friends that Roman has been keeping me captive in here since delivering Knox. That's because single women without kids do not understand how busy mothers really are. On the other hand, he could be reacting to the comment she made referring to herself as Knox's godmother. In fact, I'd bet a hundred bucks that his issue is with the latter.

We've been discussing for months whether Knox needs official godparents and if we were to pick some who'd they be. He, of course, would struggle to select between the King brothers since he adores all three of them, although I'm pretty sure it would be Camden if he had to choose. My pick would obviously be Sloan (in fact, I've always promised her she'd be my first child's godmother), although Roman has expressed to me on more than one occasion that she would be Knox's godmother over his dead body. The thing is, Sloan doesn't actually know that there's a debate about it at all. So, needless to say, I've left that conversation behind for another day.

Plus, the reality of the situation is that if anything

ever happened to Roman or I while Knox was still young, my parents or Joseph and Juliette would get custody and we both agree that Knox would be in expert hands with either of them.

"Let's just go, Sloan. I'd rather start drinking when we get to Zoe's. She's mentioned that she's going to have some sort of signature drink made with rum, and I don't like to mix my liquors."

"Smart thinking, Bitsy. That's why you're the brains and I'm the beauty."

"Elizabeth is the brains *and* the beauty. You're just—"

"Roman," I cut him off with a warning.

"He knows what I meant." Sloan scoffs. "I'm in such a good mood that nothing you say will bring me down, Roman Masterson. Your control freaky ass is just pissed that you won't be around when Bitsy gets drunk off her ass tonight."

Roman shifts uncomfortably in his seat as he shoots daggers into Sloan with his eyes.

"Be quiet, Sloan," I warn her.

"What did I say now?" She feigns ignorance. "There was nothing disrespectful about what I just said. It's all truth."

While I've long since accepted the fact that Roman and my best friend have two forceful personalities and a contrary relationship which sometimes makes moments like this funny and other times awkward, tonight their verbal sparring has me virtually at the point of tears. I'm emotionally exhausted.

"I'm leaving my son for the first time to do absolutely nothing of any real importance and all this back and forth between the two of you is seriously getting on my nerves!" I explode. "Just shut up."

Roman stands from the chaise and walks toward me in several powerful strides. He slides his hand into my hair, cradling the side of my face, and tilts my eyes toward his.

"First, Duchess, you look fucking hot tonight."

The unexpected compliment makes me crack a small smile.

"Thank you."

"Second, you're wrong. You're not going out to do absolutely nothing. You're going out to have some fun because you deserve a night out with your friends and your happiness is as important as a motherfucker."

"Exactly," Sloan adds.

I ignore her two cents and concentrate on the man I love, who at this moment makes me wish I was staying home for a little private picnic in our bedroom. We haven't done that in a really long time. Those are always so fun.

"Maybe I should stay home and just lay like broccoli with you," I say, laying my hand on his chest. "We never took that shower, I promised."

"Go," Roman says to my surprise with no reservation. Then he gives me a G-rated kiss on the lips. "If you two end up drinking too much, I'll send a car over. Have fun. Just not too much."

"Are you sure you're okay with this?"

I feel kind of pitiful that he's not putting up a fight and asking me to stay home. I really wish he would.

"I'm watching the game tonight, baby. I'm good."

"Okay," I agree disappointedly.

I listen for any sign of Knox to come through the monitors but hear nothing. He's fast asleep, and at this point I'm running out of excuses to stay home. Maybe I just need to pull up my big girl panties and leave my two men alone for a few hours.

"Ready?" Sloan asks eagerly. She hasn't been out much either since her new promotion. This will be a welcomed change of pace for the both of us. Just like old times.

The house will not blow up if I leave.

Knox will live through one night without me.

The business will not implode if I take the evening off.

I just have to rip off the Band-Aid and say the words.

"Yep, I'm ready. Let's party."

4

ELIZABETH
Two Hours Later

I slide off my sandals and try my best not to make a sound in my bare feet as I creep inside the house, but my efforts are futile. Roman is wide awake and sitting in the living room watching a movie, noshing on some takeout.

"Why am I not surprised," he says sarcastically as I cross the threshold into our living room.

"I had such a good time," I say unconvincingly.

"You were there for an hour," he deadpans.

I check my watch.

"No, I was there for two hours."

"It takes thirty minutes to get to that part of town

and thirty to get back, so you were literally there long enough to get one drink, eat a piece of cheese, and maybe say happy birthday. So what's up? Why are you home?"

"Nothing's up."

"Did you not like the vibe there? Were her friends psycho? Did some dude hit on you?" Roman's voice grows progressively concerned. "Or did a woman hit on you?"

"No, no, it was fine." I chuckle. "Zoe had the furniture in her loft cleared out and she decorated the place with balloons and soft lighting. She even had a good deejay and a candy table. It was a really nice birthday party."

"Then why are you here, Duchess?"

I look around for Knox.

"Is he still asleep?"

"Is that why you came home?" Roman asks with disbelief.

"No, of course not, and stop trying to make me feel guilty."

"He woke up for an hour, drank a bottle, and then went back down."

"Oh, so he's okay?"

"He's perfect."

"Oh."

I lay my handbag on the kitchen counter and open the fridge to grab myself a bottled water. I notice that there's a huge tray of baked ziti inside that I've never seen before.

"You ordered ziti too?"

"Nah, Jade brought it by."

"Then why are you eating wings?"

"I ordered them before she dropped by."

"What made her bring by the food?"

I might be a little sensitive about the fact that I haven't cooked a decent meal for the two of us since... forever. And now his assistant seems to pick up the slack.

"She had extra."

That's a lie.

"What single woman makes extra trays of ziti unless she's going to a baby shower?"

"I didn't say she made it."

"Whatever the case may be, it's weird."

"Jade is weird. You already know that. So what? The more important question on the table is whether you had one of those signature drinks you were waiting to taste?" Roman asks.

"A guest told me that the bartender was watering down the drinks, so I didn't want to have to toss out my breastmilk for a crappy drink. What would be the point in that?"

"So you didn't drink?"

I've never heard Roman sound so disappointed because I'm home or that I didn't have any drinks. The world must be ending. Who is this man?

"No."

"And where's the Glamazon?"

"She's still at the party."

"Is she going to be okay there?"

"I left her at a house party with friends, not a rowdy roadhouse bar," I say sarcastically. "Plus, it turns out one of Sloan's coworkers is friends with Zoe. She said she'll give her a ride home if she needs it."

"Cutter will make everyone's life miserable if anything happens to that woman."

"Ah, so that's why you're asking. I should have known it wasn't out of genuine concern."

There's a long pause between our exchanges. The air between us feels heavy with many things said and unsaid. We haven't been this communicative with each other in weeks and since Knox is asleep, this might be a good time to have the conversation that I've been putting off.

"Are you okay?" I ask him. "Like, are we okay?"

"We're always okay, Duchess."

I search for the right words to get my point across.

"Then why did you basically push me out the door when I tried to stay home tonight? Why do you always seem so disappointed with me lately?"

"Come here, Elizabeth."

"We're talking. I think I should stay over here."

"Come here," he says in a firmer tone.

Roman knows that being physically close to him is my Achilles heel. That's because being near him is always a tactile experience. His body is fit and hard, yet warm and enveloping. He smells like a mixture of clean soap, strong whiskey, and hot sauce. I can't help but wonder in amazement how he managed to fit in calling in an order of hot wings and taking a shower while watching Knox for only two hours and I can't seem to fit in eating a yogurt and taking a bird bath for three days.

"Not there," he instructs. "On my lap."

My favorite party jeans are skintight thanks to my post baby body, but fortunately they have enough spandex in the fabric that allows me to spread my legs and straddle Roman's lap. His request seems very calculated. I feel so vulnerable whenever I'm in this position with him. He could ask me to do almost anything and I would say yes.

"I want you to slow down, Duchess."

Yes to anything but that.

"What do you mean?" I ask as if I'm clueless to what's he asking of me.

He raises my eyes back to meet his.

"Admit it. You didn't stay at the party because you're completely exhausted. You were probably sitting in the corner somewhere, sipping on a ginger ale, and fighting to keep your eyelids open."

He's exactly right.

"That's not at all what happened," I fib.

"Lying was never your forte, baby." He pulls my body closer into his. "Do you know that it physically hurts me to see you like this?"

I close my eyes and snuggle into Roman's embrace, listening to the beating of his heart. Sometimes the construction of the human body amazes me. The steady rhythm of this organ is keeping the man I love most alive and is also the sound that lulls me to sleep most nights. It's a sound I pray I hear every night for the rest of my life.

"I'm fine, Roman," I say in my most convincing voice. "Trust me, I would tell you if I was drowning."

"Interesting that you use that word."

"What do you mean?"

"You said that you're drowning."

"I said I would tell you if I was," I annunciate my consonants to make a stronger point.

"Quiet," he says, holding me tighter. "Just rest."

My body curls into his, but my brain is moving a mile a minute. I can't stop it if I wanted to. There are several more things I need to do before I can just rest, but I don't feel like hearing any disapproving remarks about it. I need to pump my breasts, make some bottles for tomorrow with the milk, check some emails, wash off my makeup. Oh God, now that I think about it, I'll be up for another two hours at this rate. He'll be furious with me.

"Let's get dinner this Friday." Roman's voice rumbles through his chest. "We haven't had a date night in a while and Jade can book us something over at the new Italian place on Spring Avenue. It's family friendly so we can take the little monster with us and then maybe take him to see our bench in the park afterward?"

Roman's family date night suggestion reminds me of why I am in love with this man. He knows me so well and takes such good care of me. I'd love a night out that includes both of my favorite guys. I lean back so I can look at him in the eyes when I tell him just how much I love his idea, but he holds me, continues to hold me firmly by my torso to his chest.

"Don't move."

He pivots and lounges back on the sofa and pulls me down with him. As I lie on top of him, he runs his hands up and down my back. The beating of his heart sounds even stronger in this position and is almost hypnotic.

"Mmm."

My eyelids flutter shut as Roman lightly massages me into a deep, relaxed state. Maybe some things I was going to do tonight can wait. There's always tomorrow.

"Let's hire a full-time nanny," Roman says.

My eyes pop immediately back open.

"We have a sitter."

"You use her sparingly. Let's get someone full time."

"You know I don't want to do that. It's bad enough we have a cleaning lady too."

"But we can afford it, Duchess."

Sometimes it bothers me when Roman uses the word *we* about his money. I never thought I'd be so sensitive about our financial situation, but I guess I want financial independence more than I thought I would. It's not that Roman ever makes me feel that I have less of a say because he makes most of the money, but I am naturally prone to letting him have his way with buying decisions because it is *his* money. It drives me crazy that I feel this way, which is the very reason why I need to rectify it by generating my own income.

"You can afford to buy a private jet too, but that doesn't mean you should buy one."

There's a brief and uncomfortable silence between us. Hiring someone full time has been a long-standing point of contention since my pregnancy that we will never see eye to eye on. He thinks it's ridiculous that I won't accept any help with Knox, and I think it would admit weakness if I do. I don't need or want someone else raising my child. I can raise Knox and grow a business without full-time help. Women all over the globe do it every day, so why can't I?

"If I thought buying a jet would be a wise investment, freeing up some of my time, improving my overall health, then I would buy one."

"Then you'd be an idiot," I say. "It's an unnecessary extravagance that only speaks to your privilege."

I roll myself off of Roman's body and he releases his arms, allowing me to do so. The turn in the conversation ruined the mood for both of us. Calling him an idiot is tantamount to calling him stupid, which is something he's never much cared for.

I leave the room and go check on Knox. He's lying in the crib wide awake playing with one of his crib toys, and when he notices me leaning over the railing a smile brightens his face.

"Hey, peanut."

I pick him up and we sit together in the glider that my parents gifted us. The chair didn't exactly match the natural colors of the nursery decor, but Sloan recovered the cushions to make it work and now it's my favorite piece in the room.

I'm grateful that Knox is hungry because my breasts are swollen with milk and I need to relieve them. As I nurse him, I close my eyes and attempt to hum a song from my childhood, but it ends up turning into the theme song of a television show.

Sing me a song.

Of a lass, that is gone.

Say could that lass be, aye.

I'm a mess. I can't even get a lullaby right. I'm not sure if it's because I'm so bad at this or the fact that Roman and I just had a disagreement, but a feeling of sadness overwhelms me and tears roll down the side of my face.

I don't actually see when he approaches the room, but I can feel his presence just the same.

Roman is standing in the doorway, looking pensively down at the two of us.

"I'm sorry," I say without looking up at him. "You're not an idiot."

"You're crying," he observes.

"I hate it when we argue."

"Then don't argue with me, Duchess."

"I'm not getting a nanny and that's my last word on it."

He watches the two of us for another quiet moment.

"Get some sleep," he says.

The next thing I hear is the front door slamming shut.

5

ROMAN

I scoop a forkful of Juliette's homemade pot pie inside of my mouth and revel in the taste as I bite into a tender piece of chicken. Joseph must have saved humanity in a past life, because in this life his beautiful wife cooks him extraordinary dinners from scratch almost every night. Tonight it's comfort food. Another night it might be a lobster boil. The old man has always been a lucky bastard.

"How's the crust, sweetie?" Juliette asks, as if there was any other answer but damn good.

"Delicious."

My woman is many things, but a wizard in the kitchen is not one of them. That's why I occasionally sneak back here around seven in the evening, because I'm almost guaranteed something delicious is cooking inside or on top of the stainless-steel Viking Range I bought Juliette for Christmas three years ago.

"I should teach you how to make it. Have you ever thought about learning how to cook?"

Imagine me cooking a pot pie from scratch. Not even Mr. Tibbs would want to taste a scoop of that disaster.

"This is becoming a dangerous habit," Joseph comments as he walks into the kitchen.

"Be nice, Joseph." Juliette glides her hand along Joseph's chest and then steps out of the room.

"What's become a dangerous habit?" I ask as I continue to chew.

"You coming here for dinner."

"I guess you will never get the hang of this father thing, will you? This is my childhood home. I'm supposed to come home and visit."

"Not without my grandson with you."

"Elizabeth took him to a mommy and me swim class tonight."

"Then you should have come by here another night."

"I see how you are now." I take a swallow of my

juice and bitterly wash down my last bite. "All you care about is Knox."

"What do you want me to say? So glad you're home, Roman. Please eat all of my dinner and while you're at it stay the night in your old room upstairs and I'll read you a bedtime story?"

"Listen, old man, this is still my house too, and if Juliette invites me to come by and have a meal, I'm coming. It's obvious that she desires a little more normal human interaction than she gets around here. It's called having a conversation. You should try it sometime."

"Stop whining."

Joseph pours himself a lowball of whiskey and sits across from me at the table.

"Uh, no thank you. I don't want a drink."

"I didn't offer because it's clear you've already had a few."

He's right.

I stopped by a local bar for a drink before I came here.

"Why haven't you gotten your house in order yet?" he asks me point blank.

"I don't know what you're talking about."

I take another angry bite of my food.

"You're not fooling anyone. You're not here for

the pot pie or the chitchat. You're here because being a new father is a hundred times harder than you ever could've imagined. You're here because you can't even convince the mother of your child to slow down and marry you. Face it, you're here because you don't want to go home."

"I'm here for dinner. That's it."

"You think I don't know you've been out for a drink tonight and the last three nights this week? You're wallowing in your own misery, and for what? You have the most beautiful life a man could ask for."

Joseph is seriously pissing me off. My relationship is none of his business. I take another forkful of food and purposely chew it slowly as we eyeball each other.

"I guess coming here was a mistake."

"Have I ever given you poor advice?"

"You think telling me I'm being a pest and pitiful is good fatherly advice?"

"It's best to keep people, even Juliette, out of your relationship. You already know what you need to do to make things right. Just be man enough to go home, stay home, and get it done."

"As usual, old man, thanks for nothing. This little

talk has been super-duper, *not* helpful, and you've ruined my appetite."

I place the fork down on the table and suck my teeth.

"Since I'm your father, I feel obligated to give you at least one more piece of advice whether or not you want to hear it."

"You're shitting me, right? Your advice sucks."

"I'm a happily married man, so I think there are a few words of wisdom you could accept from me if you were smart enough to listen."

"My relationship is different than yours. It includes taking care of a new baby and a workaholic fiancée. Two things that you know nothing about."

"You may not have been a baby when I brought you to live with me but I raised you up all the same, and I didn't work my ass off half of my life for you to sit in my house and complain about your girlfriend with Juliette."

"She's my fiancée," I correct his miserable ass.

"I can understand that it scared the hell out of you when Elizabeth got hurt last year, but sometimes you have to give people the space they need to love them properly."

"You think I'm smothering her?"

"I think you need to get back to doing what you do best and that's work."

"You think I'm following her around the house all damn day? I do work, Joseph."

"You take calls, you advise, you consult, but you aren't out in the trenches working the fixes yourself anymore. You're at home, hovering. You need to leave the house and not when you're angry to go have a drink, but when you have a purpose."

"That's the worst advice I've ever heard. I have two people that need me at home. That's where I should be."

"And how is that working for you?" Joseph snickers. "You may not be my flesh and blood, Roman, but that will never matter because you and I are similar in all the ways that matter. I'm telling you that for many years, work is what fueled me, but loving Juliette is what calmed me. There is a difference between the two and you need both. You need to keep busy and stay productive or you're going to be a miserable son of a bitch to live with. You probably already are. If you suffocate Elizabeth with all of your restlessness, you'll never get her down that aisle. I promise you that."

"Who says I can't get her down the aisle?"

I take one last bite of my delicious free dinner, a sip of my drink, then I stand to leave.

Joseph simply stares at me with an infuriatingly smug look on his face. He calls me on my shit all the time and I can't stand it. Why do I keep coming here?

"Thanks for dinner!" I call upstairs to Juliette. "I'll see you on Thursday at five."

"Oh okay, hun. You're leaving already?" she asks in response.

"Yep," I reply, as I give Joseph a displeased look. "I've evidently got some thinking to do."

6

ELIZABETH

I've been sitting at my desk for most of the day working on my presentation for Cabot University when I realize that in the last three hours, I've only created one additional PowerPoint slide and have about fifteen more to go. My contact lenses have practically dried out from staring at the computer screen for so long. I decide the best course of action at this point is to take a much-needed break, especially after my stomach growls.

When was the last time I ate something?

I'm completely unfocused.

All I can think about is how tough things have been between me and Roman lately and sometimes

I wonder if perhaps we both moved too fast too soon. Our chemistry burned hot and fast, our courtship was a whirlwind, and our engagement came soon after a lot of drama in our lives. Should we have slowed down and dated longer? If we did, would we even still be together? Would we have Knox?

There are reasons why some women tell you to wait to have children. Now I understand why. Roman and I weren't together long enough or alone as a couple long enough. There was still more of "us" that we had yet to explore before we became this family of three.

I'm unsure if he feels smothered or stuck with me, but what I do know is that he's been coming home late the last few nights and I don't know where he's been or who he's been with. A part of me knows that he would never cheat on me, but a part of me wonders what he is seeking elsewhere that he cannot seem to find at home with me and Knox.

My cell phone vibrates on the kitchen counter while I'm seasoning the pieces of salmon I bought from the market. It's Sloan. She doesn't even say hello, she just starts talking, and as usual it's about herself.

"Girl, I just got off of the phone with that guy I

met at Zoe's and would you believe he gave me some totally made up excuse to back out of our date?"

"I thought you two had a vibe going at the party?"

"I thought so too. Now, suddenly, he isn't interested. Girl, maybe he's married."

"Yeah, maybe."

"It's so weird though. He's like the third guy that's flaked out on me. It's like they are all over me when we first meet and then something changes. Tell me the truth, Bitsy. Do I have bad breath? You know people never tell someone when they do. They just talk about them behind their backs."

"You don't have bad breath, Sloan," I assure her.

"You sound distracted. What are you doing right now?"

"Believe it or not, I'm cooking dinner."

"Cooking?" She chuckles lightly through the phone. "You hate cooking though."

"I don't hate it. I just don't do it very well."

"So what's on the menu?"

"Salmon with caper sauce, asparagus, and roasted potatoes."

"Aww, shoot, not only are you cooking but you're getting fancy with it!"

"It's a Food Network recipe."

"They've got mail order services for that, you know? They send you the meal practically made and suddenly everyone thinks you're a gourmet cook."

"You've ordered those types of kits before?"

"Hell, no. Any man I'm dating knows good and well that I expect to be treated out for dinner at least three times a week."

"You're so spoiled." I laugh. "Maybe that's why men keep flaking out on you."

"I'm spoiled? Everyone knows that the dark knight spoils you rotten. So what gives? Why the elaborate dinner suddenly? I thought you'd be working on that PowerPoint of yours."

"I just wanted to do something nice for Roman. Things seem a little off between us lately."

"Off in what way?" she asks suspiciously.

"I guess he's crankier than normal."

"Isn't Roman always cranky?" she asks, half-joking.

"No," I say in a melancholy voice.

"You sound down, Bitsy. What aren't you telling me? Do I need to come over there and whip some Masterson ass?"

I tear up.

It's a good thing Sloan can't see me because my overprotective friend would probably overreact as usual. Little does she know that she and Roman are alike in so many ways.

"Things are just... really hard, Sloan."

"How are they hard?"

"Things have changed between us since Knox was born and I'm thinking, what if being with me isn't what he thought it was going to be? What if loving me and Knox is harder than he expected? I mean, he's never been in a relationship this long or this serious before and my body doesn't look the same since—"

"Hold up! Let me stop you right there before you work yourself up in a tizzy. If there's one thing that I know about that control freak is that he loves the stinking ground you and baby Knox walk on. He would bribe, maim, and kill for y'all. Shit might be tough right now, but life is hard for a lot of folks.

"If any couple is going to figure it out, it's going to be you two. If I can't believe in your love, then what chance does a girl like me have? So burn up that salmon you're cooking, serve it to him in that pink lace bra and panty set I gave you for your birthday, because he doesn't give two shits about any stretch marks you might have."

"You haven't seen it lately. My butt jiggles now."

"Your ass has always been rounder and cuter

than mine, and since delivering the baby it's even better."

"I just really need him to hear me. I need us to talk to each other and not at each other."

"Wear that set and he'll listen to anything you have to say. I promise you."

I treasure my friend and her much-needed pep talk. Once we hang up, I finish up my sauce, take a quick shower, and put on the lace bra and panty set.

While the color of it pops nicely against the color of my skin, when I take a side view glance at myself in the mirror I'm not exactly in love with how I look in it. My breasts are spilling over the top of the lace cups, the waist of the panties are basically hidden under my new tummy pouch, and I feel like I'm trying way too hard by wearing this.

"What do you think?" I ask Knox as he sits in his caterpillar chair chewing on a teething biscuit. "Is it too much?"

Knox looks straight at me as he babbles a few words, then laughs. His mouth full of mushy biscuit.

"I could interpret that in so many ways, peanut." I smile. "I'll just pretend that you told me to go for it."

7

ELIZABETH

I don't know where Roman's been the last couple of hours, but I can tell when he steps through the door he's thoroughly impressed by what he smells. Frankly, I can't believe I cooked it either. It smells and looks better than anything I've ever made before.

"Is Juliette here?" he questions as he ditches his boots at the front door.

I exit the kitchen barefoot, dressed only in the pink lace bra, a pair of matching panties, and a white ruffled apron around my waist. I notice a sudden surge of lust in Roman's eyes, yet he refrains from acknowledging the fact that I'm standing before him half naked.

"Juliette's not here," I tell him. "I cooked the delicious meal you are smelling."

"Really?"

"Yes, sir." I smile brightly.

"This is a surprise."

"Are you hungry?"

"Always," he says in a playful baritone voice.

I smile at his flirtatious response and turn to get his plate ready when he notices that I'm wearing matching panties underneath the apron.

"Do you enjoy cooking in your underwear, Duchess?"

His use of my nickname makes me clench at my core. I turn around and notice the bulge forming at his crotch.

"I wanted to be comfortable," I say. "It's kind of hot today."

"Do you need any help in there?"

"No, everything's ready."

"Okay, I'm going to say hi to Knox first."

"Wait, he's not here."

"Where is he?"

"He's in Penn-Washington with my parents."

"Who's idea was that?"

He takes a seat on one of the stools at the kitchen island.

"Mine. I thought it would be good for us to have dinner alone and talk."

"Talk." He repeats the word as if it's a foreign concept.

"Yeah, talk."

"Come here, Duchess."

I approach Roman tentatively, and he pulls me closer in between his legs.

"In this bra and panties you want to just talk?"

"Yes."

"Is the food still cooking?"

"No, it's been ready for about thirty minutes."

"All right then, let's talk."

He slides his hands down to my hips.

"Maybe I should, um, sit down and then we can talk."

"Why can't you stay right here?"

"You are, um, poking me," I say while nervously biting my lip.

"Because you are only wearing your underwear, baby. Of course you feel me."

This outfit was a mistake.

At first I thought I wanted to do the whole sexy siren thing, but you have to possess an enormous amount of confidence to pull that off, even with the man you love, and right now I'm feeling the polar opposite of confident. It feels desperate.

"I really do just want to talk."

He drops his hands.

"I'm so fucking confused right now."

"I know. I'm sorry."

I run out of the kitchen and into the first floor bathroom. I put on the robe that is hanging on the back of the door and take a long look at myself in the mirror.

You tried to put a Band-Aid on a gaping hole tonight, dummy.

"What just happened, Elizabeth?" Roman asks with concern through the door.

He probably thinks I'm insane.

"I'm just tired."

"Open the door, baby."

I slowly open the door and am met with deeply concerned eyes.

"Why did you put the robe on?"

"It was a stupid idea."

"What was stupid? To cook me a delicious dinner or to surprise me dressed in something sexy as hell?"

I wrap the robe tighter around my waist, hugging myself in the process.

"You wanted to talk, right?"

"Yeah."

"I hope it was about our wedding. I'd like to marry your pretty ass before our son is old enough to ask us for the car keys, or does that ring on your finger mean nothing to you at all?"

I gaze lovingly into his eyes.

"It means everything."

"Then set the date."

"I wanted to wait."

"For what?"

"For the right time."

"The perfect time for us to become man and wife is right the fuck now."

"Maybe once I lose a little more weight."

"You are the most beautiful woman in the world. Your new curves make my dick applaud every time you enter a room. You better not lose another fucking pound, Elizabeth, and I want your wedding dress to hug your hips, ass, and tits properly. I want everyone to see what a prize I've won and how I'm the luckiest fucking man on the planet. You're not my girlfriend or my baby's mama, Duchess, you are my life and I want to make this legal for the world to see."

I'm having a full ugly cry at this point.

My ob-gyn said that there would be tons of hormonal fluctuations after the pregnancy, I just thought I was past them all. I've never cried this much in my life.

I can tell that my tears are shredding Roman, so he does the only thing he can think to do. He unties my robe, wraps his hands around my waist and lifts me gently onto the bathroom counter. He grabs a wad of toilet tissue and dabs at the tears rolling down my cheeks.

"Shh," he tells me. "You know I hate it when you cry."

He slides his hand down the side of my face and traces a line down my clavicle and to my breasts. He bends over, gingerly placing a kiss on the tops of each one. He then slides the robe off of my shoulders and unfastens my bra.

His eyes lustfully dance as he watches my large mounds jostle free from their captivity. A small droplet of milk flows from one of my breasts and he quickly dabs it dry with some tissue and several soft kisses. I close my eyes in rapture as he suckles gently back and forth around each nipple making sure not to suck to greedily.

Roman pulls me down off the counter and places me back on my feet, permitting the robe to fall completely to the floor. He turns me around to face the mirror above the sink and pulls me back into his embrace.

"Look at us," he tells me. "There is no more perfect moment than every moment that we're together."

He sucks on two of his fingers then slides the hand down the front of my panties, slipping those two fingers in between my folds on either side of my clit. I lay my head back on his chest and close my eyes because it feels so frackin' good.

"Open your eyes, Duchess. Watch as I make you come. Remember who you belong to."

I lazily open my eyes and look back into the mirror. The reflection of this gorgeous man and his tatted arm diving farther into my pussy is so hot I can feel myself gushing onto his fingers.

"So wet," he says approvingly in my ear.

He continues his rhythmic stroking of me as he takes his other hand and wraps at the base of my throat.

"Play with your tits for me, Duchess," he orders.

"Fuck, you're beautiful."

I'm panting with need as I pluck my nipples.

I'm getting so close.

"You ready to come, baby?" He smirks in the mirror.

"Yes."

"How badly do you want me inside of you right now?"

"Badly."

"Then you know what to do."

He wants me to beg and at this point I'll do whatever he wants so that I can come.

"Please fuck me, Masterson."

His eyes look crazed with desire for me. His grip stays steady around my throat as he uses his fingers to pinch my clit with just the right amount of pressure that creates sparks of white lights behind my eyes as I climax.

"Eyes open!" He orders in the middle of my ecstasy, and I watch myself as I free float from my orgasm into a series of smaller aftershocks.

He kisses my back for a moment, then slides me to the side to wash his hands.

"I hope you enjoyed that because there will be no fucking you raw until you set a date, Duchess."

Wait, what?

I'm still speechless as he saunters out of the bathroom like he just proved some point. He shuts the door behind him, and for a moment I think he's walked away, but then I hear him lean against the door after a heavy exhalation.

"I think I'm going to go back to work with the guys, Elizabeth."

My stomach drops from his unexpected announcement. This is the first time he's ever mentioned wanting to go back to the club or to the fixes or whatever the hell he's talking about. I mean, how long has he been considering this?

I thought making us dinner and connecting on a physical level could help us get back on track, but Roman feels like he is drifting away from me more than ever and I don't know how to bring him back to shore.

I briefly clean myself up and open the bathroom door to face him.

"That's great," I reply, lying through my teeth.

He watches me with a deafening scrutiny as I head back to the kitchen.

"That's all you have to say about it?" he asks.

I wash my hands and lay his lukewarm salmon dinner on the table.

"What day do you start?"

8

ROMAN

For most of Knox's life, including when he was in Elizabeth's belly, I've worked from home. The new and improved Roman fields calls from potential high-end clients and if I think they're a good fit, I pass the jobs on to my partners, the King brothers. Now that their brother Stone is also working full time with us, there's no need for me to be present at every fix, but after the last few nights at home, I realize that Joseph may be on to something. I may frustrate Elizabeth, because I'm simply frustrated with myself.

"Yo, look who's here in the motherfucking house!" Cutter exclaims in his usual over-the-top fashion as I walk into the office of Club Lotus for the first time in months. "What did we do to earn the distinct honor of your presence?"

"I was in the neighborhood and thought you might need me."

"Need you?" Cutter laughs. "For what exactly?"

I realize he's only breaking my balls, but the rhetorical question stings. I know I haven't been as hands on this past year, but this is still my business. A business that my friends have deeply benefited from.

Camden stares silently at me, no doubt trying to read my body language. He's the master of that. He always reads the room and assesses a situation before diving into it with words or action unlike his little brother. Stone doesn't make any snide remarks either, but walks over to shake my hand.

"Good to see you, man."

"Same."

"Seriously, what's going on?" Cutter asks. "You good? Everything okay with Elizabeth and Knox?"

"Would I be here if everything wasn't okay with my family?" I respond, probably a little too defensively.

"Oh, true dat." Cutter smiles. "I guess you wouldn't."

"Heard you've been to Milo's club this week."

Camden's comment sounds judgmental as hell.

"For a drink."

"And what magical liquor do they pour at Milo's that you couldn't get here?"

"Nothing but a twelve-year-old single malt whiskey with my name on it."

Diving into each other's private business is not something that we do, so they simply respect my answer and we move onto another topic of conversation.

"It's good you're here. We got that information you wanted on Elizabeth's friend," Stone says. "I followed her like you asked, and she's definitely got a problem over there."

Elizabeth explained that the woman she sent a thousand dollars to is an old college friend who needed the money to move because her landlord was harassing her, but later was planning on returning it because the prick wouldn't accept her thirty-day notice. In fact, he only grew more aggressive after she tried submitting it. So when she asked me if her friend might have any legal recourse against the landlord, I assured her that involving the police wouldn't be necessary and that I could handle it with a brief conversation. It's just one less thing I need Duchess to worry about.

"What's his deal?" I ask.

"He's clean as a whistle. Credit score good. Owns three of the apartments in that community. No record. Not even a parking ticket," Camden says.

"No one is that clean."

"I will say this," Stone adds. "He rents most of his apartments to women that fit a very similar description. Young, pretty, short, blonde, and they're all students."

"So he's creating his own built-in dating service."

"The dickhead's a predator," Cutter says. "Plain and simple."

"So what are you going to do?"

"He's going to have to be dealt with."

"What do you mean dealt with?"

"Elizabeth mentioned her friend is from Oregon, so she's a long way from home with no family here to speak for her. So I'm going to pay the little prick a visit."

"Who are you, Batman?" Cutter asks flippantly. "Now you're out here defending helpless damsels in distress?"

"Keep it up, fathead."

"I'm just saying, Rome. We pay assholes a visit

when we're getting paid for it. What you're thinking about doing is something we did when we were seventeen. Kid shit to impress a girl."

"Yeah, man, I spent a week's worth of time and resources tracking that dude for you. I thought there'd be some payoff."

I look at Cutter and Stone like they've lost their minds. Are they fucking serious right now?

"This is different and you know it," I try saying calmly.

"Because it's for Elizabeth?" Camden asks incredulously.

"Fucking right!"

I stare down every King brother in the room. Each one of them bigger than the next. No one was more happy than me when Camden and Cutter found their brother Stone, but right now their collective brotherhood asses are getting on my nerves. I ball one of my fists tightly, ready to swing, if one of them says one more thing about this favor or Elizabeth.

"Look, he's ready to swing on one of us!"

"*Dayummm*, we were just busting your balls," Cutter says as all three of them bust out into deep belly laughs.

"Y'all weren't lying," Stone says. "I thought he was going to slit our throats."

"Can I get you a drink?" Camden asks facetiously. "Because you look like you need it."

"Is this a frat house?" I say snidely. "Did I just get hazed by three jackoffs?"

They continue laughing like I've just said the funniest shit ever.

"Is this what you three do all night in my club?"

"You mean laugh?" Cutter asks sarcastically.

"Whatever," I mutter under my breath, recognizing that they got me good. Things have been so tense lately, I can't even tell when my oldest friends are messing with me.

Finally, I crack a smile.

I guess it was kind of funny.

"Hey, so we've been working on the job Kat gave us," Camden says, getting serious for the moment.

"How's that going?"

I grab a scoop of M&M's out of the dish on Cam's desk and take a seat. It's starting to feel a little like old times when we would hash out the details of a fix over drinks and junk food.

"I don't know, Rome. It's way messier than she described, and it's going to take some muscle to clean up. Maybe more than just the three of us."

"Well, now there's the four of us," I say. "That's why I'm here."

"Whitfield is still stuck in Chicago and they have told him not to return home to Miami because he's their number one person of interest in the case. They've got eyes on him twenty-four seven."

"That means they're building a case."

"Yeah, it's definitely a shit show. Accident or not, he killed that girl and left his prints all over the goddamn apartment. They're probably just dotting their i's and crossing their t's at this point. They're going to make an arrest soon."

"What about our political connect in Chicago? Maybe he could help lose some of that evidence."

"Nope, Washington is up for re-election," Cutter says. "And he won't touch this case with a ten-foot pole. We offered him ten stacks and he wouldn't take it."

"He wouldn't take a ten-thousand-dollar campaign donation?"

"Turned us down flat."

I continue to try to troubleshoot.

"Cam, can't you make the prints go away with a few clicks of a mouse? Isn't everything stored on an online database?"

"Doesn't work like that, my friend. First, I'd have

to break through the Chicago PD firewall and then I'd have to erase a million different digital footprints so it wouldn't trace back to us."

"What's your friend Kat paying us for this job?" Stone asks.

I guess Cam and Cutter don't share everything yet with their long-lost brother.

"Enough," I say.

"Enough to risk Cam breaking into the police department's database?"

"Hell no," Cutter chimes in.

"Was she a sex worker?" I ask, trying to figure out an alternative solution. "Maybe we can pay off the witnesses in the apartment building."

"Negative. She was a dental assistant he met at a hotel bar. The girl's family already has a GoFundMe campaign up, collecting money for the case and demanding for the killer to be brought to justice. The prosecutor's office is going full throttle on this," Stone responds. "The girl was an innocent."

"Should we pass on this one?" Cutter asks. "I thought we were going to get celebrity clients like Mendez from Kat, not messy ones like this."

"Clients like Mendez are not fixes, they're babysitting jobs," I say. "I'm learning that we're not going to get a lot of those types of jobs. People hire us to fix the messy shit."

"Yeah, and just because a job is a little more complicated doesn't mean we're going to pass. Kat is paying us a lot of money to get Whitfield back to Miami, and that's what we're going to do. We're just going to go old-school to get him out of there," Camden says.

"So we have to knock a few heads around," I say matter-of-factly. "Like the old days."

"Exactly."

Cutter is right about one thing. I promised that we wouldn't take on a lot of risky clients like this anymore, but that's because Kat made me certain assurances too. She said she'd give us cushy fixes for her celebrity clients in Miami. This one is a lot more complicated and could end up being one of those cases we call a barn burner or in other words there will be casualties.

"We don't know how long we must be there, Rome," Camden says. "Maybe you sit this one out and help on the next project?"

"Yeah, what about Elizabeth and Knox? You've got a lot more to lose than we do, brother."

Both Camden and Cutter are bringing up an excellent point. Just because I want to jump in balls deep and get back to work doesn't mean I want to be risking my neck over seven hundred miles away from my family.

"You three go. I'll ask Joseph if he can find us a few hired hands if you need extra muscle in Chi-town. He definitely has connections there. I'll manage the day-to-day stuff here."

Camden nods his head. "That'll work."

"Plus, you've got that kid you need to frighten over in Drexel Village," Stone says with a smile.

"Shut up." I laugh. "You're getting as bad as they are."

"Feels almost like old times." Cutter laughs. "Welcome home, Rome."

Yeah... I guess I am home.

9

___

ELIZABETH

"**W**here's my grandbaby? Mimi Juliette is ready for some serious face time with her baby today."

My aunt glides through the doorway and into our living room, dressed as always in effortless glamour. She's wearing a pair of breezy wide-leg khaki slacks, a crisp white T-shirt, her hair is smoothly pulled back in a low bun, and gold hoops adorn her ears to finish the look.

Excited energy is practically humming off of her. She's never been able to have children of her own and so being a hands-on grandmother (fondly known as Mimi) to Knox has been like a dream come true for her.

"I'm super glad to see you but I didn't know you were coming. I'm afraid I have plans today."

"I know you do," she says, as she playfully raises and lowers her eyebrows. "That's exactly why I'm here."

"I'm sorry, but I think you and I may be talking about two very different things. What plans are you talking about?"

Aunt Juliette walks over to the high chair and picks up a very overstimulated Knox. I sat him in the chair to calm him down, but he's been banging on the tray table ever since I placed him there. She struggles to lift him free from his seat because of his height and girth. They definitely build these chairs for the average-sized baby and not a child as large as Knox.

"He isn't buckled in but let me pull out the tray for you. That'll make it easier for you to lift him out."

"No, hun, I've got him."

Knox is as solid as a rock and I can practically feel a twinge in my own back watching Juliette continually try to lift him free.

"Got him! Ooh, he's getting so chunky. I love it!"

she exclaims, as she pecks a kiss on Knox's cheek. "He's the most scrumptious baby ever."

Knox babbles several strings of nonsense words in what I believe is an attempt to have a full-blown conversation with her.

"And then what?" she says to him with bright eyes.

He babbles some more and she laughs in response.

"Is that so, Knox? You are so smart."

The two of them are definitely in love with each other. It's actually really sweet.

"So, Auntie, what plans are you referring to?" I ask again to get the conversation back on track. Knox has a way of distracting everyone who comes across his path. He definitely possesses a magnetic energy that draws people in. He reminds me so much of his father in that way.

"Don't you and your husband talk to each other? He told me to be here today at five on the dot."

I purse my lips.

"Five o'clock for what?"

"Obviously, for whatever you're doing this evening. Isn't it date night?"

Roman and I haven't had date night in weeks, but I get why he's trying. We've been out of sync lately. I work and take care of Knox all day, and now he's back at the club all night.

"He really should have checked with me first before he made any plans."

"Then it wouldn't be a surprise. Joseph does things like that for me all the time. I guess those two become more alike with each passing day."

Juliette miraculously tosses my big baby in the air, and he squeals with delight as he soars up and then back down. I'm not sure how she lifts him that high without straining a back muscle or ending up looking like a mess. I feel like I have a dull lower backache and smashed Cheerio dust in my hair at all times.

"He thinks I'm working too much," I confess. "He thinks I need some additional help around here."

Juliette tilts her head and gives me a long look in the eyes.

"Well, now that you mention it, maybe you do. You do look a little tired. No offense, sweetie."

"None taken." I guess. "What gave it away? My dark circles?"

"If it makes you feel any better, I've read that most new mothers are sleep deprived for at least a year and don't even realize it. How much sleep do you think you get at night?"

"I don't know, maybe four or four and a half hours a night."

"Four hours? Oh no, dear, you're going to need at least double that. I don't have kids or an exciting business like yours, and even I still need eight hours of rest."

"Uh, eight hours will not happen. Eight hours is laughable. I can't even recall the last time I slept a full eight hours."

"This little pumpkin won't leave you alone, huh?"

"He's always hungry." I chuckle. "Can't you tell? He's the biggest baby on the planet, or at least in the pediatrician's office."

"Do you take him to all his checkup appointments by yourself?"

"Sure."

Aunt Juliette takes a seat on the couch and cradles Knox in her lap. I notice him eyeballing one of her earrings, but before I can warn her about his earring obsession, she continues with her inquisition.

"Hmm, so it's true. Roman mentioned that you won't allow him to help much with the baby.".

"No, it's not true," I say defensively.

I decide to change the subject.

"Oh, goodness, I forgot to offer you something. Would you like anything to drink? I could get you a Diet Coke or some of that herbal tea you like."

"No, dear, I was just wondering if perhaps you could let Roman do a few more things to support you."

It's obvious that she will not let this subject go. Maybe that's her true purpose in stopping by. There probably is no date. I'm thinking the grand plan was for Juliette to conveniently drop by and tell me all of things I'm doing wrong in this relationship.

"He takes care of the dog," I deadpan.

I take a moment to rub Mr. Tibbs's belly. It's easy to forget that he's in the room sometimes because he's such a good boy. He never snaps or snarls when Knox tugs too hard at his tail or ears. He just licks him in the face and then goes to lie down in a corner somewhere to stay out of the way.

"Mr. Tibbs practically takes care of himself. I was thinking more like having Roman take Knox to his next well visit or have him handle some solid food feedings so you can rest."

"Knox doesn't eat a lot of solid food yet."

"Hmm, really? Could that be why he's so hungry? How long are you planning to primarily breastfeed?"

Oh, she's definitely been talking to Roman or worse... my parents.

"As long as he wants to," I say defiantly. "It's good for him. He's getting all my antibodies and all the nutrients he needs. I've read extensively about it."

"Of course, dear. I was just trying to help troubleshoot things."

"Troubleshoot what exactly?"

I'm feeling attacked by this conversation, but Aunt Juliette doesn't even bat an eye and continues on with her line of questioning.

"Elizabeth, Knox is eight months old. You've been engaged and living with Roman for well over a year. When are you two going to get married?"

"You're not the first person to ask me that lately." I sigh.

My parents have asked repeatedly about it, my old assistant Blake mentioned it when he emailed me last, and even someone at Zoe's party complimented me on my ring and asked when the big day was.

"Well, it's a perfectly legitimate question. This is the longest engagement in our family's history." She smiles.

Aunt Juliette's attempt at a joke falls on deaf ears. My parents have made it quite clear how they feel about me living in sin "for no good reason" and I'm not about to appease their conservative ridiculousness by booking a wedding date at a church I don't attend.

"I don't want a church wedding. We don't even go to church."

"Then what kind of wedding do you want? I could help you with the planning if you want."

"A Vegas wedding."

"Vegas?" she replies with a distinct tone of disdain in her voice.

"Yes."

"Like the kind of wedding with Elvis officiating?"

Although my aunt is considered the black sheep of the family, I don't think she realizes just how much of my family's elitist middle-class ways she still harbors.

"And if I had Elvis officiate would it be a problem?"

"Have you told your parents about this?"

"They are aware and they hate the idea just like you apparently do, but I have my reasons for wanting the wedding in Las Vegas."

"May I ask what the reason is?"

"There's a special guest who will attend who lives there."

"You mean Roman's mother?"

"Yes."

"I want Roman to connect with his mother more than anyone, but what about your guests who live here? Do we all have to fly to Las Vegas to accommodate her?"

"My guests can afford it, so yes. If anyone in the Hill or Masterson family chooses to be a part of our special day, then they will have to fly to Las Vegas."

"But you can also afford to fly Frances here as your special guest. I don't get why you have to inconvenience everybody else. She wouldn't want that."

Roman and I made a bet that if either of us guessed the sex of the baby correctly, that we'd be granted one wish from the other. Getting the Masterson Made tattoo highlighted in blue was part of my gender reveal surprise. Even I didn't know I was having a boy until Zoe showed me the design when it was halfway completed. So since I guessed the sex correctly, the wish I requested was for us to be married in Las Vegas so we could invite his mother as our special guest. He hates that it binds him to our agreement because his relationship with his mother is quite complicated and it makes him uncomfortable, but I will not cave.

I realize that it's a risky request. His mother

doesn't have the best track record and we would be putting the ball entirely in her court to show up, but I seriously doubt that she would miss her only son's wedding, especially if it's hosted in the city where she lives.

"I'm sorry, but this is something Roman and I decided a long time ago and if we're going to be honest, you have no idea what Roman's mother would want."

"Well, I guess there's no need to get into a debate about the theory of a Vegas wedding right now anyway, because the way you're moving it's not happening anytime soon. I mean, you haven't discussed a potential date at all and weddings take months to plan."

"No, we haven't locked down a date as yet, but I've been a little busy with the company and raising this little stinker. When the time comes to plan, you'll be the first to know."

I bend over and kiss Knox on the nose.

"Okay, then why don't you tell me about School Bucks. Could Roman possibly help in some capacity with the business so you can start planning this Vegas wedding?"

Just what in the ham sandwich has Roman *the*

snitch been sharing with Juliette? She is like a dog with a bone today.

"Uh, no, he can't. Just like I can't help him with his business."

"You have a new important client, right?"

Unbelievable.

"Did Roman tell you what I had for breakfast too?"

Juliette laughs. "Instant oatmeal with bananas?"

"Oh, my God! Since when have you two been best buds and having all these brief chats about me?"

"It's not like we talk about you all the time. Just a few times."

"All the time when?" I ask, totally confused.

"When he comes by for dinner."

I swallow the lump in my throat.

"He comes for dinner a lot?"

My aunt shifts her feet uncomfortably because she clearly thought I knew.

"Well, he hasn't been lately."

Now I'm embarrassed that it's obvious that I don't know where Roman is half of the time. I thought perhaps he'd been at the club with the Kings since he recently returned to work, but now it seems as if he's been going by to see Juliette and

Joseph too. It almost seems like he wants to be anywhere but here.

"Elizabeth, understand, I've never seen Roman act like this about anyone ever. He only comes to talk to me out of concern. Loving you and Knox is very new for him, just like it is for you. He had you all to himself for a good while and now he has to share you. He just wants to protect and love you both the best way he knows how."

The chasm between Roman and I is a little more complicated than what my aunt just described, but it's not something I want to discuss with her. I have too much on my plate and with this possible university contract on the horizon; I need to keep my energy high and focused.

"Did Roman really make plans for tonight, because he's going to be very disappointed if he can't change them. I have an important meeting tonight and it's probably going to run late because of the time difference with some participants."

"He definitely had something planned, but I truly don't know what it is. I'm just here to watch Knox while you two do whatever it is you end up doing. Those were my instructions when he came by for—"

My aunt stops mid-sentence.

"Came by for what?"

"Pot pie."

Jerk.

He didn't even bring me any leftovers.

"And Elizabeth," Juliette continues, "before you two wander completely off course, I'd cut the man some slack and reconsider taking part in whatever he has planned. It seems to me like you both need it."

My smart watch alarm dings just in the nick of time. I'm totally over this conversation. I guess I really had no idea that everyone in my life was going to have such strong opinions on how I mother my child, run my business, and manage my relationship. I'm through explaining myself to everyone in my life about why I do what I do, especially Roman. Not to mention that date night has always been Friday nights, not Thursdays.

Gah!

"Oh, crap, I forgot all about the call that I need to take before my meeting. It's a good thing you're here. The sitter isn't coming until six."

"Cancel the sitter. I'm here for the entire day and I can't wait to have my little grandbaby bean all to myself."

Knox calmly lays his head on Aunt Juliette's

breast and starts playing with one of her gold earrings. He looks utterly content and it makes me think my little boy has a thing for boobs with or without milk, just like his daddy.

"Aww, he's so adorable," she says as she rhythmically pats Knox's back.

"Watch it," I warn her. "He has an earring fetish and those look expensive."

"It's fine, isn't it, Knox?" she asks in a hushed tone as she continues to pat him. "You will not do anything to Mimi's anniversary hoops, will you?"

Knox sighs heavily and continues to play with her earlobe. He really is an easy baby once you give him what he needs. Food, a dry diaper, and affection. That's all my little peanut needs. I don't know why everyone's so worried that I can't take care of my boy without all this help they claim I need.

"You two look like you're going to be just fine."

"We will be."

"Okay then, there's a bottle in the fridge if Knox gets hungry and his favorite book is on the bedside table in his nursery. I'll be in my office until I hear from Roman. Thanks for this, Auntie."

"It's my pleasure. That's what grandparents are for."

Even though it's clear whose side Juliette is on, I

feel a little more at ease that she'll be here when Roman arrives home instead of the sitter. Maybe it's because there's always this low level of tension in the room when we're together lately. Maybe it's because I know that he will not be happy when I tell him that I cannot take part in whatever he has planned tonight. If he had just mentioned it earlier, I could have told him that today wasn't a good day.

But he rarely asks.

He just decides, and they seem to always conflict with my own.

Not to mention that nothing I do is ever good enough for him these days. He wants me to sleep more. He wants me to work less. He wants me to fuck him more and breastfeed my son less. Everything he wants is at complete odds with what I want... except for making love.

That I would love to do.

But when I attempt to think about anything remotely sexy, it's two o'clock in the morning, I haven't showered, and my breast ducts are filled with milk. What the frack is sexy about that?

After my call with one of my app developers in Bangladesh, I quickly throw my hair up in a messy bun on top of my head, change into a clean shirt and shorts, and apply some lip gloss. This will be my third video chat with the president of Cabot University, and I'm finally allowing myself to become excited about this project.

A magna cum laude graduate of Yale, he's the youngest president in Cabot's history and is so open to innovative ideas. I really think I have a strong chance of making School Bucks bigger in the collegiate space with a man like him making decisions.

"Lovely to talk to you again, Miss Hill."

"Same here, President Maxwell."

"I'd prefer it if you called me Jacob. My father was a president of a bank and so he's really President Maxwell."

"Okay." I giggle. "If we're ditching formalities, then you should call me Elizabeth."

"Perfect. So, Elizabeth, I wanted to see if we could talk dollars and cents."

"Sure thing. What are your questions?"

"Well, in your estimation, what would it cost to integrate and promote School Bucks on our web platform? I want to give students the opportunity to apply for scholarships straight from their personal dashboards."

I do my best not to smile too widely and give away the fact that I am elated that he wants to make a bigger commitment. My one goal from this meeting was to negotiate a live link to our website from their scholarship page, something that would have been a major win for us, but to have complete integration with their student backend? That would be amazing.

"Well, to be honest with you, I didn't run figures for such a large roll out. I thought you'd only be referring the app to students not wanting a partnership with us."

"Let's think bigger, Elizabeth. The School Bucks application is a great idea and long overdue. I don't want Cabot graduates in vast amounts of debt when they walk out of our doors. I want them to easily access free grants and scholarships available to them so they can graduate from this university without tons of loans to worry about. I just recently paid off all of my student debt from graduate school five years ago, so I totally understand this. Implementation of your app will be transformational for some students, and it is in direct alignment with the university's strategic plan."

I'm floored.

I'm elated.

I can't wait to tell Roman about my meeting.

"I'm so excited, Mister—" I accidentally revert back to addressing him formally. "I mean... Jacob.

Thank you for the opportunity. I promise you won't regret it."

Without a knock or any warning, Roman appears in my doorway dressed deliciously in black from head to toe. His sudden presence startles me and as my head whips around to face him, my messy bun falls out of the ponytail holder and curls fall wildly down and around my face.

"You're welcome," Jacob continues talking through my computer screen, not realizing that anyone has entered the room. "And may I just say that you have some beautiful curls, Elizabeth?"

Uh oh.

10

ELIZABETH

I keep my eyes pinned on the brooding man I love in the doorway. I'm ashamed to admit it, but this is probably the first time in weeks I've truly taken a long look at him without being distracted by a call or the baby or whatever.

He is the sexiest man on planet earth. He hasn't shaved in a few days and has a five o'clock shadow covering his square jaw, and his tattoos look especially bright as they pop against the black tee he's wearing. He is out of the view of the computer's camera, so Jacob doesn't know he's there, but to me it feels like Roman is in every crevice of this room.

"Could you hold on one second, Jacob?"

I mute the sound on our video call without even waiting for a reply.

"I'm in a meeting," I say to Roman as gently as I can.

He's in a mood.

I can feel the waves of disapproval rolling off of him, so I need to wrap things up with Jacob quickly before I get into any sort of a verbal joust with him.

"I can see that."

"So... I'll be finished shortly. Is everything all right downstairs with Aunt Juliette and Knox?"

"Of course it is," he replies with a little more bass in his voice than usual. "Why wouldn't it be?"

Roman doesn't move from where he's standing, and it doesn't seem like he's planning to. He just stares at the computer screen with malice emanating from his stormy obsidian eyes. I take a deep breath, turn around, and do the only thing I should at this point, unmute myself, and end the call quickly.

"So, Mr. Maxwell—"

"Ah, how soon we forget. It's Jacob, remember?"

"Right, I forgot that fast." I smile painfully. "Jacob."

Roman slides one of the spare folding chairs I keep in the office abrasively across the floor. I do my best to ignore the fact that he has probably caused irreparable harm to my beautiful oak floors and that Jacob can also hear the ear-splitting sound.

"Pardon me, but I just remembered that I have another call with one of my developers overseas. This is the only time he can talk because of the time difference. Would you mind terribly if we pick this up later? I'm so sorry."

"No need for apologies, Elizabeth. School's out for the summer, so my load is a little lighter than normal. We can reschedule later in the week. What day is good for you?"

Roman takes a seat in the chair and scoots himself closer to the view of my webcam. This is so embarrassing. I literally feel like wringing his neck.

"Hello," Jacob says with a friendly tone now that he notices Roman sitting next to me.

I kick Roman's calf with my bare foot so he'll acknowledge Jacob's greeting. I forgot that he does these crazy leg exercises that make the muscles in his calves feel like bands of steel. It's no wonder that my toe throbs.

"Hey," he responds tersely.

I don't bother with any introductions because I'm mortified. Could he be any more unprofessional? I mean, this is the president of a whole damn university I'm trying to close a deal with.

"So, um, let me get back to you on the date and time later today, Jacob. Is there any day that doesn't work for you?"

I imagine that Roman looks quite ominous dressed in his simple black T-shirt and black jeans to someone like Jacob. Right now he's crossing his muscular arms across his chest, showcasing the intricate sleeves of custom ink that adorn both of them. This is all a ridiculous show to passive-aggressively let Jacob know that "my man" is in the room. He might as well pee on me.

"I'm in meetings all day Wednesday but any other day will work. We just have to sync our schedules," he replies.

"Okay, in the meantime I'll have my team send over a few projections of what we hope a complete Cabot and School Bucks integration would look like and estimates on cost."

Jacob nods his head in agreement and opens a large calendar on his desk. He leafs through the pages looking for the best time for us to speak again and I feel like I'm making a colossal mistake. The entire point of this virtual call was to get a commitment from the university today, and now that he wants to give it to me, I'm getting off of the phone for what? Because I'm embarrassed that my fiancé is acting like an asshole?

"You know what, can you hold on for just another moment, Jacob? I think I may have figured out how to rearrange a few things and clear up my schedule so we can chat a little longer."

"That would be perfect. I'll answer a few emails while I wait. Take your time."

"Thank you so much for your patience."

I mute the audio once again and adjust the monitor so we're both out of the line of vision of the computer camera.

"Roman, can I speak to you outside, please?"

"Why can't we talk right here? He can't hear us."

"Roman, I'm not asking."

I stomp defiantly outside of the office and into the sitting room, which is one of my favorite rooms in the house because Sloan decorated it so beautifully. It's a peaceful space decorated with clean lines and muted colors, plus, it's the sunniest room on the second floor. I like to sit here when I'm reading a novel or just want a quiet moment away from the rest of my life.

After a long defiant pause, Roman follows me into the room and stands silently against one wall, staring at me as if *I've* done something wrong.

Typical.

"I'm having one of the most important business calls of my life in there and you are acting like—"

"I'm acting like what?"

"A jealous brat."

He scoffs as if my comment is ridiculous. "Why would I be jealous when you're already mine?"

"I am my own woman and I have been for a very long time or haven't you noticed?"

"You are *my* woman because it says so in blue ink, above your hip, and underneath those shorts."

"Oh, stop it. Just what the hell are you doing? Jacob is the president of a university. I am trying to create a partnership with him. He clearly is interested so—"

"Yes... he clearly is."

Roman slowly cracks the side of his neck, a telltale sign that he is losing patience with this conversation, but I don't give a damn. I am one hundred percent right on this one. I won't be bullied.

"What is that supposed to mean?"

"You two are already on a first name basis, he complimented you on your hair and not your ideas, and he definitely looked at your ass when you stood up from your chair just now."

"All you can see is a person's ass when they stand up and turn around!"

"Especially when they're wearing running shorts at a business meeting."

"He was only supposed to see me from the neck up. I had to stand up and turn around because of you!"

"That's another thing. Why isn't this is a regular phone call? Why do you have to talk to him on a video chat?"

"Where is this coming from? I have virtual calls all the time. Would you rather me leave you and our son and drive clear across the state to go meet Jacob in person?"

"Now you're just being a smart-ass."

"And you're just being an ass."

"Am I?"

"Yes, you are, and I'm tired of it. In fact, I'm utterly exhausted. You're exhausting the hell out of me."

"You want to know what I'm tired of?"

"I'm dying to know. What could you be possibly tired of?"

"I'm tired of the excuses."

"Excuses! Please elaborate."

"You're too tired, you're too busy trying to be

everything to everybody, and you're *always* on the most important business call of your life."

"You freakishly tall jerk! I just carried and delivered your colossal, ten pound son eight months ago, thank you very much. So yeah, I am tired and I am busy. Hell, I'm frackin' supermom. I should get an award for bringing your child into the world. They should name a Medal of Honor after me!"

"And what does giving birth to our love child have anything to do with being too busy to marry his father?"

"What did you say?"

"Or have you just conveniently forgotten about the big-ass diamond promise I put on your finger?" He points resentfully at my hand.

Roman has never mentioned having a problem with us putting the wedding on hold until today, and to be honest, I haven't given a vast amount of thought about it. We love each other. We're raising our son together. I thought we were fine to wait until things settled down in our lives. I assumed we were on the same page.

I have been consumed with all the growth in the business and with being a new mother. I'm not even sure how it happened. It's not like we formally discussed waiting, but we just never really started planning. I want to marry him. He is my forever after. He and Knox are everything to me. How could he think this is some sort of avoidance issue for me?

Dammit.

The moment I realize that I've totally forgotten that Jacob is patiently waiting to finish our meeting, Roman recognizes it on my face.

"You can call him back. We're talking."

"I can't just leave the president of—"

"I don't give one flying fuck what rinky dink college he is the president of."

"Well, I give *all* the fucks."

"I'm warning you, Elizabeth."

So maybe now I'm pissed too. Some of his points may be valid, but Roman is being unreasonable, and that man knows how to push all of my buttons both good and bad like no one else in the world.

I stroll over to the mirror, slide my hands into the roots of my hair and fluff my curls a bit. I add some moisture to my lips by giving them a long lick and then I flippantly say to him, "Be right back, baby daddy."

I'm crystal clear that I've now officially pissed him off.

"Elizabeth, don't go in that office."

"And what are you going to do if I do?"

"I doubt that you want to test that."

"This is not a test," I say sarcastically. "I repeat, this is not a test."

I stroll back into my office, sashaying my hips exaggeratedly as I do. I lock the door behind me and take a seat. Jacob is still there, working on his computer, and pops his eyes back up when he sees me.

"All good?"

I unmute myself.

"Yep."

"Great, I sent you an email that you can look at to help with cost projections."

"Wonderful, I'll take a look right now and we can—"

CRASH!

The frame to the doorway of my office suddenly splinters into several large pieces.

Roman—and my door—has literally become unhinged.

11

ROMAN

I haven't had pussy in thirteen days.

Or a night of uninterrupted sleep in eight months.

I could go on and on about the reasons why, but the bottom line is that I'm breaking down this motherfucking office door because I've had enough.

Sometimes physicality is the only way people understand me. Powerful people pay me an obscene amount of money to clean up their mistakes, which is not a cakewalk. You can't just knock on the door of the attorney general and tell him to overlook the accidental murder of a young woman by the CEO of a billion-dollar entertainment firm.

First, I have to convince him to let me inside the door, then I've got to hope he is amiable to being paid off, and if he isn't, I may have to threaten him with bodily harm. You'd be surprised at how many times people don't take the money. So I'm not afraid to admit that I've had to crack a couple of skulls and point my gun at someone's temple more often than not to get the job done. Aggression can be an effective motivator, especially when it's sexual and consensual.

"Roman!" Elizabeth yells.

She's half startled, half pissed, and totally sexy.

"Elizabeth, are you all right?" I hear a concerned voice from the computer monitor.

"She's fine," I say succinctly for his benefit.

I lift my tee up over my head, toss it behind me, and take both of my forearms and use them to slide everything on top of Elizabeth's desk to the floor including her computer with the full screen of president "who gives a fuck" university. It sounds worse than it really is when everything comes crashing down to the floor, but making all of that noise is sort of the point.

Now I have her full and undivided attention.

"Did you just break my eighteen-hundred-dollar computer!"

"I'll buy you another one."

"There are words for deviants like you."

I stealthily move toward my woman with a mixture of determination, frustration and want. I miss Duchess like crazy. It's incredibly sad to me how we see each other every single day, but we haven't connected in what feels like forever.

"Spontaneous?"

"Crazy."

"Crazy for you."

"No, just batshit crazy."

"I promised you a long time ago that you would always pay a price for not listening to me, but the upside is that you're going to love every minute of it."

Elizabeth's eyes widen with just a smidgeon of lust until she catches herself. Then her face returns to the vexed look it had before.

"I'm not in the mood to play with you, Roman."

"Really, because your tits are leaking milk all over the place."

She looks begrudgingly down at her top. "They do this all the time."

"They do that when you're horny or when the baby's crying and the little monster isn't here. I had Juliette take him for a stroller walk into town, so common sense tells me you're horny just like me."

"Fucking you is the very last thing on my mind right now."

"Let's see how much of a lie that shit is."

I stalk closer toward her and let my dick lead the way. He's pointing right in her direction.

She raises her hand up. "Back away, Neanderthal."

I don't listen, but just keep moving forward as she backpedals her pretty little ass to the farthest corner of the room.

"Sticks and stones, Elizabeth."

There's an ottoman in the room she forgot about and almost trips and falls backward, but I leap forward and catch her around the waist just in time.

"Got you," I mutter in her ear.

"I hate you right now."

"Do you, baby?"

"Yes," she lies in the most deliciously breathy voice. A voice I know all too well. It's the sound that practically hums in my ear when I'm deep inside of her.

I'm still holding onto her as I slide a hand down the front of her favorite pair of navy blue running shorts. A pair she often wears around the house when she's working. Her cotton panties are soaked right through to the crotch of them.

"You hate me so much but you're so fucking wet that I could slide my entire fist inside of you."

"That's disgusting. Shut up."

She shoves my hand away and I almost laugh out loud as her eyes dart from left to right, no doubt worried that someone is listening to our conversation. He isn't though. The computer cord pulled out of the outlet and the glass screen now looks like a spider web.

"That attitude of yours is going to get you into all sorts of trouble today," I promise her.

She rests her hands on her hips, ready for confrontation.

"And so is yours. Do you realize all the explaining I'm going to have to do to Jacob about your juvenile behavior?"

"Call him Jacob one more time."

She glares at me with a formidable scowl.

"I'm warning you, Duchess."

"Jaaacobbb," she repeats slowly and succinctly.

My jaw twitches at her defiance. I know that she's trying to push me as a punishment for embarrassing her, but there's something more going on that is broadening the chasm between us. Her perfectly innocent business conversation with that man bothered me more than it ever should have. Her fighting me on every damn thing lately is irritating me more than ever. The fact that she won't set a wedding date is really pissing me off too. So I guess the only solution I feel is left to be heard by her is through physicality.

Through sex.

It is our one common denominator.

I wrap my hand around the base of her throat right as she's annunciating the last *b* of his name and pull her into my body. The pressure I'm applying is slightly tighter than I usually use.

"You're going to regret that," I say into her skin.

She bites the corner of her lip and looks at the missing office door.

"What are you looking over there for? Nobody is home. Nobody is going to see what I'm about to do to you and your juicy hot pussy. Correction, *my* juicy hot pussy."

"Roman."

Yes, I definitely have her attention now.

She's so used to us getting interrupted by the baby, a phone call, or the cleaning lady that I think she's forgotten what's it like to be completely and utterly consumed by me.

I'm going to have to refresh her memory.

12

ROMAN

Still gripping Elizabeth at the base of her neck, I guide her back across the room to the empty desk. I use my available hand to bend her at the hip and twirl her around facing the desk. As my other hand pivots around, holding her by the back of her neck, I push her forward and bend her over the desk.

"Place your arms above your head and grip the edge of the desk."

Elizabeth lies purposely motionless on the desk, so I give one of her ass cheeks a smack.

Whack!

Her disobedient ass doesn't make a sound, not of

pleasure or pain, but what she does do is exactly what I instructed. She slowly brings her arms around and holds the edge of the desk with her fingertips. Of course she complies. Elizabeth loves it when I do anything to her from the back. That shit turns her on.

I reach down and yank her shorts and nerd-sexy pair of cotton panties down to her ankles. I'm eager to pay homage to her new "after Knox" curvy body. I hungrily kiss her rounded hips, her full ass, and the backs of her thighs while taking inventory of the body that used to belong to me every night until my little monster robbed me of my time.

She doesn't make a sound.

Not one.

She's using every bit of restraint she has left to defy me.

She looks breathtaking in this position, stretched across the desk in a ninety-degree angle, but I completely step away, leaving her bare ass exposed to see if she'll move or leave. This would be the perfect opportunity for Elizabeth to end this encounter between us. If she doesn't want me, if she doesn't need me as much as I'm desperately craving her, then I'll surrender.

But she doesn't move an inch.

Not one.

Thank fuck.

"Spread your legs but don't step out of the shorts," I order, now that I feel emboldened to move forward.

Her breathing becomes a bit shallower as she obeys my command. I lick the corner of my mouth in anticipation and approval. Elizabeth looks spectacular from the back and keeping the shorts around her ankles will create a nice bit of tension as I lick her clean.

"Take off your top and bra."

Slowly, she peels off her T-shirt and bra and tosses them in front of her on the floor. The fact that she is following my direction calms me. This right here is exactly what I need and what she wants.

I return to the warmth of her soft body and this time take my time using my hands to travel up her bare skin, following the length of her back, massaging and kneading the tight muscles there and along her neck.

My woman spends long days at the computer working on her business, and it's one reason I'm so drawn to her. Her work ethic is sexy. Her desire to win is intoxicating. Wanting School Bucks to succeed and hustling all the time to make it a reality is part of what defines her, and I understand that. She has something to prove to her parents, her classmates, herself, and maybe even to me. She wants to show us all that she can turn her dream into a thriving reality and that she doesn't need anyone's help to achieve it.

But if there's one thing that I've learned from watching Joseph and Juliette's relationship, it's that there has to be a balance. Where there is darkness there must be light, where there is intensity there must be calm, and it's my job as Elizabeth's forever after to remind her of that. To remind her of us. I want us to win in both business and love, and it only works if we're doing both together.

"You're beautiful, Duchess. Absolutely beautiful."

I can feel her body relaxing under my touch, but she still doesn't utter a single sound. She doesn't want to give me the satisfaction of knowing that she is enjoying every minute of this, especially after how I left her in the bathroom the other day. She knows that I totally get off on her responsiveness to me.

Yet even with no verbal communication from her, there's still something very gratifying about watching my woman do what she's told, bent over, looking gorgeous as hell, and holding onto her desk wearing nothing but a pair of shorts around her ankles.

I step back again and allow a moment of silence to pass between us to appreciate the view.

The quiet unnerves her.

I've been making love to her for a long time now, studying her actions and reactions both in and out of the bedroom, and I know she becomes most uneasy when she doesn't know what's coming next or when it's coming.

Elizabeth adjusts her posture by repositioning her legs and bringing them slightly together and tilting her body a little higher on the desk. Her muscles are probably tiring of the position I placed her in, but that's exactly why I put her there and why I'm keeping her there. I need her to be present in every moment of this.

"Don't let those shorts touch the floor. Spread your legs apart."

She exhales harshly but does what I've requested. Her compliance satisfies a savage part of me, yet my resolve is slipping too. I wanted to wait a little longer to give her the pleasure I know she desperately craves.

I know what I said before. I wanted to wait for her to ask for it, to beg for it, but I've got my own desperate desires clawing inside of me and it's been entirely too long since I've been in between my woman's legs.

So fuck making a point.

I drop reverently down to my knees on the floor directly behind her. My face close to her ass. I rest one side of my face on one of her ass cheeks and tap the other gently with my hand. A few light slaps, one after the other, directly on the same area. I can feel the vibration of the thumps against her butt and it gets me stiff as a board knowing that her want for me is growing.

"Don't move your legs one inch," I speak into her skin. "Keep those legs spread and those shorts tight around your ankles."

While there's still not one single moan from Elizabeth's stubborn ass, I know better. I am systematically breaking down all of her resistance. A few more minutes and she'll be speaking in tongues... and so the fuck will I.

"You ready?" I tease.

I slide one of my fingers through her puffy folds from back to front and feel that she's drenched. Her desire is practically pouring out of her like a faucet at this point.

"Wet as fuck."

"Be quiet."

"You keep telling me that."

"Because you keep talking."

"Oh, I can fix that shit right now."

I shove my mouth in between her legs which are still tautly spread apart and suck hard on her clit. She instantly slams her palms on the desk and her legs buckle. Her reaction makes me chuckle and the rumble of my laughter against her core causes her to slam her hand again.

I knead her ass cheeks with both hands as I continue devouring her from front to back. I run my tongue viciously back and forth across her clit like a human vibrator and relish her sweet smell and tangy taste. Then reluctantly I pull away, licking my lips as I savor every swallow.

"Delicious."

13

ROMAN

Every lush curve on Elizabeth's body makes her look like an extraordinary piece of art as she presses her fingertips into the edge of the wood for dear life, her lips slightly parted, her eyes glazed over. She's the most exquisite woman in the world, especially when aroused. When she finally releases a noise, that's a cross between a moan and a whimper my dick becomes rigid with eagerness.

Now we're getting somewhere.

"Did you say something?" I taunt her with a satisfied grin.

I whack her ass once to watch it jiggle, then flip

her around on her back. Her cheeks are ruddy, her hair looks wild like a halo of angry curls, and her nipples are tight and hard like diamonds. She looks aroused, but at the same time she also looks like she wants to spit in my face.

"Ready to come for me, Duchess?"

Her only response is a chilly death glare.

"Yeah, you're ready," I say arrogantly. "You can step out of those shorts now."

With a flick of her ankle, she kicks the shorts and panties angrily across the room and I pull her hips forward with the same ferocity, then lift and rest her legs on my shoulders.

I blow lightly on her cunt.

Kissing. Blowing. Priming her for what's coming next.

Things start to quickly progress from there as she unintentionally squirms her hips.

"Who do you belong to?" I demand.

She bangs a closed fist on the desk.

"Whose pussy is this?"

She moans reluctantly.

"You're going to have to ask for it if you want it," I tell her through a low growl, trying to keep what's left of my manhood because actually, I'm calling her bluff.

If she doesn't beg me to fuck her soon, I might explode all over her stomach like a horny teenager. My dick is so hard that if I bang it against the side of this desk, it might break the fuck off. I'm not sure how much longer I can play this game of chicken with her. This is the first time that Elizabeth might literally have me by the balls.

"No."

Okay, well, at least she's responding with actual words. That means her resolve is breaking. I'm close. I just have to try a little harder.

I take one long lick of her pussy with my flattened tongue and just when I'm about to lift my head to end the connection; she slides her hands onto the back of my shorn head and pushes me back down.

I smile to myself.

Almost there.

"You're going to have to say the fucking words," I speak between her folds.

"Roman."

The way she says my name makes my dick angry. It wants relief. It wants her. Things make so much more sense when I'm inside of her, and there was a time she felt the same way. When the hell is she going to put us both out of our misery?

"Yes, Duchess?"

"Fuck!"

Why is she fighting this so hard?

"I'm so mad at you."

"I know you are, baby, but I told you I'd buy you another computer."

"That's not it and you know it."

I exhale an exaggerated breath.

"I'm waiting, Elizabeth."

Please, dammit.

"Fine."

"Fine?"

"Fine. I'm saying the words. I want it," she says with monotone inflection.

I use an open hand and slap her wet pussy hard with one swift motion.

"Hey!"

"You can chill with the theatrics, Duchess. You're not fooling anybody. You're wet as hell right now and you want me just as much as I want you. Now ask for it the right fucking way or I'll tie you to this desk for the rest of the night and go make myself a sandwich."

"You wouldn't dare."

"Still waiting," I say, as I gingerly pull and roll

her clit with two of my fingers. She raises her hips in response.

"Okay, you win."

"What do I win?"

"Please... I... want, I need you to fuck me, Masterson."

Now we're finally getting somewhere.

"When?"

I unbuckle my belt.

"Now."

"Where?" I growl eagerly.

"On this desk."

My dick is furious with all of this foreplay, making the crotch of my jeans feel compressed and damn near painful. I unzip myself and my cock forcefully juts out, ready to get to work.

"How?" I grit the last question through my teeth.

"Hard."

Thank fuck.

I return my mouth back in between Elizabeth's legs and ravage her pussy until her body tightens hard like a drum. It doesn't take long for her to unleash.

"I'm coming!" she exclaims almost painfully.

Her orgasm rocks her hard as her entire body contorts to its release. Her back arches into a perfect bow and her eyes roll to the back of her head. She's never looked more beautiful, and I don't think I've ever been more desperate for this woman in my life.

I stand up with her hips and ass in my hand and quickly enter inside of her soaking wet, clenched walls.

My refuge.

My home.

My favorite place on earth.

It's been so long that we've been with each other like this, without caution, and with a pure abandonment that I can almost hear her pussy asking me where I've been and what took me so long to return.

Elizabeth finally relinquishes her anger to the moment and clasps her full breasts as I bang the hell out of her pussy.

"Did you miss me?" I ask through punishing strokes.

"Roman—"

"Yes, baby?"

"I think I'm coming again."

"Not yet, Duchess."

"Fuuuuck!"

"That mouth is getting out of control." I grin sinisterly. "I can't have you raising our son with a mouth like a sailor. I'm going to have to fix that shit right now."

I pull myself completely out of her, and the look on her face is priceless. She looks like a kid whose best friend just stole their toy and skipped down the street. Her cheeks are the perfect rosy hue as she continues to pant from need as I back away from her and sit in the recliner in the room's corner. I make sure not to take my eyes off of her as I remove each stitch of my clothing and sit buck naked on the chair, with my legs spread wide, and my hands clasped behind my back.

She hungrily eyes my angry cock, licking her lips, as she hops down from the desk. She lowers herself down on her knees in front of me, sliding her hands up my thighs, to my waist and then my chest as I silently watch. She takes a moment to slowly trace the new ink I had done when Knox was born. A black hawk in flight with his name spelled in a serif font along one of its wings.

Elizabeth kisses that tattoo and continues her exploration of me, finally circling her arms around my neck and pulling me down low toward her face. She kisses me with the kind of dominance and want she hasn't shown in a very long time. I run my tongue leisurely inside of her mouth, reveling in the softness of her lips and the taste of her tongue.

She breaks off the kiss by slapping the side of my face, shoving me back hard in the chair, and giving me a glare that's a cross between annoyance and lust.

Whoa, that shit was hot.

I didn't see that coming.

14

ROMAN

"I'm a grown woman and I'll speak to you in whatever way I want to."

The slap to my face sends a zing straight to the head of my dick and I ejaculate a small amount of pre-cum. While it's obvious that parts of me are enjoying this new Elizabeth, I will not let her get into the habit of trying to top me from the bottom.

That's not how this shit works.

Yet before I can even think of an appropriate reprimand, she slides her arms back down to my dick, fisting and pumping it several times. She slides her mouth down and around my shaft as her beautiful eyes stay connected to my surprised ones.

I am now deaf, dumb, and blind.

At this point, I can't formulate a complete sentence and if she keeps this up I'm going to come before she even has time to get started.

My chest rumbles with pleasure as my woman continues to work the base of my shaft with her hand and the top of my dick with her mouth. When she releases one of her hands and starts using it to pleasure herself between her legs, I know for certain that my next orgasm is going to be epic.

A delicious feeling of need and desire coils inside of me and to stave it off I fist a large clump of Elizabeth's curls to get her to slow her pace before I bust. She refuses to relinquish control though and continues sucking me so hard that before I can stop myself; I come with a powerful moan of release.

"Yessss, baby!"

She sits back on her heels, evidently proud of herself, and wipes the corner of her mouth with her finger, making sure to swallow every drop of me.

"Now finish what you started," she teases with a smile.

Elizabeth is a man's perfect wet dream. Her skin is flushed and her eyes are twinkling with the desire of a wanton seductress as she continues to rhythmically play between her legs.

That's when I see a glimmer of hope.

When we eliminate all the distractions and it's just the two of us left? I finally see that the woman I love with every breath in my body is still here. I pray that she can still see me too.

"Who's in charge here?" I ask with faux indignation.

"You are."

"Doesn't seem like it."

"I'm just asking you to be a responsible human being and finish what you started." She continues deep massaging her clit.

"How do you want me to finish?" I ask, unable to take my eyes off of the intoxicating way she is pleasuring herself.

"Hm, let me think."

I smirk at her playfulness with me.

"You on the desk," she describes.

"Uh, huh."

I fist myself.

"Me on top."

"I like the sound of this."

"Riding you."

Her hand moves a little faster between her legs.

"Yes, and?"

"Until I say stop."

"Done."

I stand swiftly and swoop Elizabeth up, cradling her ass and hips as I carry her over to the desk. Once we become comfortably adjusted on the hardwood, I slam her hips down on my length and we both hiss from the instantaneous connection of me being inside of her again.

She bends forward and wraps her arms around my neck as she works herself up and down my dick. I'm thick and stiff and it's been a while for us, so I allow her to control the tempo as her body becomes reacquainted to my size.

It doesn't take long for her to pick up speed quickly since she is sopping wet and already halfway to her next orgasm. I just make sure to have a tight hold of her ass so she doesn't fall as she bounces wildly up and down my length.

I can feel another orgasm coiling down my spine and tightening my core. This is not the norm for me. Usually I can go for a very long time before I come, especially a second time, but I'm not surprised by how fast and hard they are coming today. It's been weeks since I've been inside of my woman and my dick is ecstatic about it.

"I love you, baby," I say in earnest.

Elizabeth tilts back, working my length at a different angle like a fucking pro.

"I love, *aah*, you too."

I can't hold off any longer and growl something totally incomprehensible as I come hard.

"This pussy is amazing... *argh!*"

"Masterson," she says on an exhalation as she comes tumbling after me. Falling completely forward against my chest in blissful exhaustion.

"I was going to take you out on the boat tonight for a sunset cruise but this was a much better use of our time," I say peppering the side of her face with kisses.

"While that sounds nice, Roman, I had two major calls tonight. In fact, I need to get ready for the next one. A better night for it would have been tomorrow."

"The captain was booked tomorrow."

"Yeah, but Friday nights are date nights."

"I didn't think it mattered."

"I'm just saying that you should have asked me first."

"Are you still mad?" I ask, confused as hell.

"Yep."

Damn, I didn't fuck it out of her yet?

"You worry too much. Rest assured that you will still have the contract with Cabot University. Your boy was practically jacking off at the idea. He loves it."

Her posture stiffens.

"I guess we'll see."

I pull back to look directly at her.

"What do you mean by that?"

"I mean, we'll see if he still wants to do business with me once I go there next week."

I almost drop her juicy ass on the floor.

"Go where?"

"To Cabot."

"So you're going to leave me and Knox and go miles away to take a preliminary meeting in person?"

"It's not preliminary. He's ready to sign a contract. I just have to complete some numbers for him."

"You're not going any fucking where."

15

ROMAN

I didn't mean for that to come out as authoritarian sounding as it did, but my response is visceral to her announcement. I just fucked her well, I feel like we're finally connecting again, and five seconds after she comes she wants to talk about leaving?

"I'm going, Roman."

She wiggles herself off of my lap and looks for the box of tissues I knocked on the floor. She grabs a few and wipes between her legs. It almost feels as if she's trying to completely wipe the last thirty minutes away.

"What are you doing?"

"I'm looking for my panties."

The casualness in her voice irks me. It lacks warmth and feeling. It doesn't even seem like she's present in this conversation or that she wants to be. It's like she hate-fucked me and now she's trying to make the great escape.

"You know that's not what I'm talking about. What the hell are you doing to us right now?"

Elizabeth places her hands on her hips in a defiant stance.

"What am *I* doing?"

"It damn sure isn't me."

"Is that so? Well, let's see, you always complain about me working and you may have just sabotaged my chance of getting a six-figure contract. You think I'm a bad mother and you definitely think I'm a terrible girlfriend. You go out every other night and I don't know where you are or who you're with, yet on the other hand you seem to like to keep tabs on my every move."

"That's not true."

"Which of the things I said isn't true?"

"All of them!"

"If I don't pick up my cell phone when you call, you're two seconds away from calling a SWAT team to come find me."

She knows why I worry when I can't reach her. I have been involved with some very dangerous people and I would never want her to be a casualty of my choices.

"And you don't respect the business I'm building because you think it's some sort of housewife hobby. Something to keep Elizabeth busy when she's not having your babies, right?"

"That's not fucking true."

"It's totally true!"

"All I asked you to do was get some help with Knox and marry me. How have you turned that into me wanting to sabotage you? I'm your biggest damn cheerleader."

"You have so much faith in me, huh? Is that why you want to buy me clients?"

"I want to help you grow your business."

"So that I can stop working so hard and pay more attention to you?"

"Isn't that what every business owner wants?"

"No, Roman, it's not."

I stare at her like we are from two different planets. What she is saying right now makes little sense to me. The whole point of working hard and making your money now is so you can enjoy it later.

"Joseph and Juliette spend a better part of the

year traveling together because that's what you do when you can finally slow down. They are enjoying the fruits of his labor together."

"They only started traveling after he handed the business over to you, not while he was building it."

"You want to do it on your own, whatever the hell that means, then fine. If it will make you happy I won't mention the shit again. Ever. Okay? What in the ever loving fuck do I need to do to make you happy?" I explode with emotion. "Tell me word for word so I don't fuck it up anymore."

"Let's stop. You're too angry for this conversation right now."

I briskly rub both my hands across my head and roar from pure frustration.

"Do I make you happy, Elizabeth?" I try saying in a calmer voice to show that I'm not being irrational.

"What is that supposed to mean?"

"Are. You. Happy."

"Are you saying that you aren't?"

"I'm asking the damn questions, not you. Why can't you ever answer me with a straight answer anymore? Why are you so damn combative?" I raise my voice.

"So now I can't disagree with you?"

"Hell yeah, you can because you do it all the goddamn time."

"Where have you been going these past few weeks?"

I step closer to her to make sure my ears haven't deceived me.

"Work."

"Before you said you were going back to work."

"Oh, you mean after all the times when we had a conversation like this?"

"So you're blaming me for whatever it is you're out in the world doing?"

"Whatever I'm doing?" I ask, insulted by whatever she's inferring. "What the fuck is it do you think I'm doing?"

Her eyes drop to the ground.

"I don't know."

I feel a huge knot form in the pit of my stomach when I notice Elizabeth starting to wipe away a few stray tears with the back of her hand. This is the second time I've made her cry. I feel disoriented. Like a ship that's lost its way because the compass has been broken. She either is furious or truly doesn't trust me, and that is something that I don't know can ever be fixed.

For the first time, I'm afraid that I truly may lose her.

"When do you plan on going to Cabot?" I ask in defeat.

"Soon."

"How far is it?"

"A few hours by train." She stops sniffling and finds her bra and shirt and puts them back on. "I'll stay the night and I'll take Knox with me."

I take a deep breath and make sure I ask my next question with no bass in my voice. I'm not trying to be combative, but what she's suggesting makes little sense. It feels like she's abandoning me.

"Why are you taking Knox?"

"I'm breastfeeding. It'll be easier if he comes with me."

"Can't you just pump some bottles and leave him here with me?"

"Pumping enough milk is just too hard for me. It's better when he just takes it from my breast."

"And how's that going to work when you're there to have a meeting? What are you going to do with Knox?"

"I'm sure the sitter would go with me for a few days, or maybe I'll ask Aunt Juliette if she wants to help. She's always looking for an opportunity to spend time with him, and Knox loves her to death."

My reaction is emotional but after the last few weeks, not to mention the last few minutes in this room, the thought of Elizabeth leaving to take a meeting right now sets every hair on the back of my neck at attention.

"Now's not the right time," I tell her.

Elizabeth's spine straightens.

"I'm sorry, but what?"

"Now's not the right time to go. You're not going."

"I wasn't asking for permission, Roman."

I look around the room at the ramifications of our lovemaking. The entire contents of her desk are strewn around the room. Our clothes are askew. Her computer screen is cracked. And all of it a direct reflection of the current state of our relationship.

In total shambles.

16

ROMAN
Present Day
The Warehouse

"That's for my son, *mudak*." My female captor practically spits on me.

The Russian word she just called me isn't on my short vocabulary list, but I damn sure can tell that it ain't a compliment. She can rest assured that the feeling is mutual.

The woman's two minions are standing behind her, reveling in my injury. The quiet one is smirking at me while the boot kicker is visibly laughing.

"You're going to regret that," I promise all three through gritted teeth.

"You'd really be better off if you would just tell me what I need to know before you bleed to death in here because I don't do regrets, Mr. Masterson."

"You and your son are going to be full of them very soon," I guarantee her.

Contempt for me rolls off my captor in waves. She hates me just as much as I now hate her. While I rarely hurt women, I am ready to give myself a hard pass with this one. At the bare minimum, she's got an ass kicking coming to her. I don't care how old she is.

"Perhaps you should be more worried about the future of your wife and little boy in this picture."

I cringe at the thought of this psychopath getting her hands on my family, but her new threat doesn't frighten me as much as it ignites me. I may not make it out of this concrete prison in one piece but I will make damn sure that the three of them don't make it out of here at all, because I promised Elizabeth that the violent parts of my business would never inter-fere in our private lives, and I will keep that promise with my last dying breath.

"I'll give you five minutes to consider your options or perhaps I need to send my two associates to pay your little family a visit. I bet the wife would be more agreeable to our questioning, as women often are. She's exactly your type, isn't she, Sergei?"

"Da," the quiet one responds, looking at me with diabolical eyes.

He just raised his spot on the "gonna get fucked up" list once I free myself from these restraints.

The only good thing about this exchange is that the woman is making mistakes. Now I know at least one of their names, Sergei. I also have a good idea on where these three are from. If they are indeed Bratva, and I think they are, they are from one of the big families in Maryland. There's a slight twang to the woman's accent that sounds very familiar to the DMV area.

I desperately use the five minutes my bitch captor has given me to scan the room for anything I can use as a weapon, but there is nothing in this room, so now I must negotiate.

"Half a million," I say. "I'll give you half a million dollars to walk away from this."

"Only a half million as reparations for humiliating my son?"

"Yes."

"Is that all you think my son is worth?"

"That is what I'm prepared to offer you."

"I just spent that much on a shopping spree in

Milan." She scoffs. "You insult me and my family, *mudak*."

"Take it or leave it."

"I must commend you on your tenacity, Mr. Masterson, but unfortunately your offer is not accepted. You have three minutes to tell me what I need to know or Sergei here will make another baby with your precious woman tonight."

"Fuck you, *sooka*."

I spit out one of the last remaining Russian words I have left in my arsenal. It means bitch and I say it with a ferociousness that I pray doesn't get lost in translation.

"Two more minutes or I'll put a bullet through your temple and end your—"

WHOOSH!

Suddenly there is a sound of shattering glass. An object the size of a baseball flies through a tiny and filthy corner window that I missed earlier. Glass shards fall to the ground and there is a flurry of activity as the object tossed inside emits a thick layer of stifling smoke.

The smoke lights my nostrils on fire, but I welcome it. I know this type of pain well. Those degenerates are finally here.

The foreign object is a Cutter King special. A

messy, loud, and obnoxiously obvious chemical smoke bomb. There's absolutely nothing stealth about his bombs, but he's been making them since high school and always looks forward to the rare instances when he can set one off.

This is the perfect occasion for one.

The woman coughs and her enforcers try covering her with a jacket and move her toward the exit when suddenly there are gunshots being fired on the door handle.

"I'm in here!" I shout out in a voice strangled by pain.

My bitch captor breaks from her protective huddle and comes running back toward me, her heels clicking across the concrete a mile a minute.

"Remember what I promised," she says with bloodshot eyes. "Your family will never be safe."

I don't expect what comes next.

Her tightly pulled eyes are clouded with smoke and crazed revenge. She doesn't care that this may literally be her last breath. She shoots me at close range and right in my gut, smiling the entire time she pulls the trigger.

This is her avenging and protecting her son because that's what family does. And as I feel myself slipping out of consciousness, I vow to myself that I will not die on this cold-ass floor for the same reason.

Before today, I lived my life like death was never a possibility. I was so preoccupied with being right that I lost sight of what truly mattered. Elizabeth and Knox are my entire universe, and I will ruthlessly fight to protect my moon and star.

That is my one job.

To fight for them.

That's why I refuse to die today.

If only I could keep my goddamn eyes open.

17

ELIZABETH

During the first fifteen minutes of being in the president of Cabot University's office, I can tell that the man is seriously considering whether or not I've been a victim of domestic violence because of how our last call ended. To be fair, I am being rather quiet and tentative but not for the reasons he is thinking.

My emotions are a brew of anger and anxiety. Roman decided to spend the majority of the night out without as much as a text to let me know what his plans were or to check in on his son. I'm not surprised. He's been spending more time at the club or at Joseph's or wherever the hell else he goes, which is why I've made the executive decision to take my trip to Cabot.

So far this visit has been full of surface pleasantries, tea service and a tour of the university but I can tell that Jacob's eyes are filled with pity. I wouldn't be surprised if he wants to check me for bruises and refer me to a good therapist, but gratefully he keeps our conversation light and totally on topic so I roll with it.

"Cabot is a gorgeous campus and it's so great that they have online access to a lot of Penn's courses," I admire.

"Yes, our students are getting an Ivy League education at a fraction of the cost."

"I love that."

"But even that cost is a burden for many students, which is where your app comes in."

"Exactly," I add. "College should be affordable for everyone who wants to attend."

We walk up a wooded trail behind one of the field hockey fields. I didn't realize just how out of shape I've become. I guess sitting at a computer all day is the new bacon. Jacob doesn't acknowledge the embarrassing fact that I've become winded, but he conveniently stops and points out a few of the buildings on campus to give me a chance to catch my breath.

"And this is Berger Hall. It's the student activity center and main dining hall."

"Burger hall?" I chuckle. "That's cute."

"Berger with an E, not a U." Jacob smiles. "Mr. Ronald Berger donated five million dollars to the university upon his death. Part of the land the university sits on was donated by his family in the 1940s."

"Wow." I feel a little embarrassed that I didn't do my homework and know that already.

My cell phone dings with a missed call from my friend Patricia. She called me yesterday as well, but I truly feel that Roman and I did all we could do for her. At this point, all she could want is more money, which is a favor I'm not doing a second time.

I place my phone's ringer on silent and slide it inside my purse as we start walking again. I ask Jacob something that's been on my mind since I arrived.

"If you were to do things all over again, Jacob, would you have attended an Ivy League college?"

"Why do you ask?"

"Just taking this tour makes me realize how many wonderful universities there are that students don't have a clue about. This seems like a place I would have really enjoyed."

"I'm not going to lie, at seventeen I would have chosen an Ivy League again because I thought that was important to say on résumés and in interviews; but if I were my age now, inside of that seventeen-year-old body, I would definitely have attended somewhere like Cabot. Ultimately, it only matters that you get the degree and a decent education not where it's from."

"That's easy for us to say though, huh?" I smile.

"True, but that's what I honestly believe. That's why I accepted this position. I hope to be a part of making Cabot a lot of students' first choice school."

I look at Jacob's left hand and notice there's a platinum wedding band on it. I consider how my life may have looked differently if I had ended up with a man like him, someone who understands my background and my mission because he grew up similarly and wants the same things. Maybe Roman and I are too different. Perhaps that will always be our problem.

Roman barely said a word when Juliette, Knox and I left in the morning for the train station. He had the driver put our bags in the car as he watched us silently from his chaise. He said his goodbyes to

Knox the night before after watching an episode of *Sesame Street* and playing with some food based finger-paints, but the two of us were barely speaking.

It took only a few moments of silence on our ride to the train station for my chest to tighten with sorrow and for Juliette to finally address it.

"It breaks my heart the way you two just parted from each other."

Knox's head tipped to the side and his eyes closed. Being in motion knocked him right out.

"He basically ordered me not to go as if he has any power over what I do or don't do."

"And you're going, anyway?"

"Are you listening to yourself, Aunt Juliette? Yes, I'm going. This is business."

"Roman isn't the type of man to stop you from growing. He isn't that petty."

"Yet that's exactly what he's doing. I'm thinking—"

"What are you thinking, sweetie?"

I looked over at Knox and was afraid to say the words out loud. I didn't want to put them in the air. I didn't want the universe to think for even a second that, that's what I wanted, but I said it anyway.

"That we are not a good match for each other anymore. That we made a mistake."

"Nonsense." She slapped the top of her thigh for emphasis.

"You saw him back there. Six months ago he would have never let me leave without holding me and saying he loves me."

"And how about you? I didn't see you say goodbye either."

I said nothing in response because everything she said was accurate. I was being just as stubborn as Roman, but that's because I'm right.

"Just don't let too much time go by without rectifying this, Bitsy. You can never get back time lost. Trust me, I know."

Once Jacob and I arrive back to the main administration building, we head to his office where there's a small spread waiting for us that includes a variety of deli sandwiches and chips. There's still a rather enormous elephant in the room that I decide I should squash now. I'm not sure exactly how much Jacob heard, but I know that I probably need to say something or this entire meeting is going to be excruciatingly long.

"So I wanted to explain what happened the other day."

"Oh?" He pretends as if he hasn't the faintest idea of what I'm referring to.

"When we lost connection."

"Oh, yes. One minute you were there and the next you weren't."

"My fiancé accidentally pulled the power out of the wall, and then my son needed me." I'm not sure if he knows that I'm lying through my teeth, but I hope it's a plausible enough excuse for us to move on. "That's why I didn't get right back to you."

"No worries, Elizabeth. I thought it was something like that."

Our meeting gets back on track and I am showing Jacob a cost analysis of the app's implementation on a budget spreadsheet I created when I feel my cell phone vibrate for the first time in about an hour. It better not be Patricia again, I think to myself, but it's not.

It's Jade.

And when I check my notifications, I see that there are thirteen missed calls from her.

"I need to take this."

"Sure."

I grab my phone and head out into the hallway.

"Hello?" I answer with an attitude. How dare Roman use his assistant to communicate with me when he couldn't even say two words to me this morning.

"Bitch!" Jade is crying hysterically. "Why didn't you pick up the phone?"

A foreboding chill covers my skin. Jade is not the emotional type. Something must be very wrong.

"What is it, Jade?" I ask reluctantly. "What's wrong?"

"It's Roman."

"What about him?"

A tear rolls down my face in anticipation of whatever she's going to tell me. I know whatever it is isn't good.

"They shot him, Elizabeth. Those fuckers shot him."

At first, I can hardly breathe.

Next begins the uncontrollable watering inside of my mouth.

And now I've finally thrown my entire lunch up.

Jacob finds me on my knees, crouching in pain, and covered in vomit.

"My God, Elizabeth, let me get you a doctor."

I wipe my mouth with the back of my hand and look up at him through tear-filled eyes.

"No, Jacob, I need to go home now."

And then I pray to God for a miracle.

18

ROMAN

I can smell the salty waters of the Atlantic Ocean as I glide down the coast in my yacht. The sun reflects off the side of Elizabeth's face in a way that makes her look almost ethereal. She's never looked more happy and it makes me feel like a superhero knowing that I put that smile on her face. Then there's my son. He's jumping with joy in his favorite car bouncer toy that he loves. Not a care in the world.

Oblivious to the subtle rock of the waves, Elizabeth continues to beam as the staff serves us a sumptuous brunch, and after the night of fucking we've had, we need to replenish. She dips her pinky finger in a small bowl of applesauce and slides it inside Knox's mouth. He abruptly stops his jumping and savors the fresh taste. His reaction to food entertains me. He's a boy after my own heart. I can't wait for him to try a peanut M&M one day. The perfect food. He's going to love them.

As the ship takes a slight turn toward our destination, I realize something. I don't know where the hell we're going. I don't remember giving the captain a destination plan. Are we going north to the Cape or are we headed south toward Miami? I have real estate in both places. I just don't remember what we decided.

I open my mouth to ask Elizabeth if she remembers where we're headed, knowing damn well that she's probably planned some child friendly outings wherever we're going, but... I can't.

This is not like me.

Something is strange.

Every time I try to open my mouth and ask her a question, she can't hear me. Why can't she hear me? My heart feels like it wants to burst outside of my chest and not in a good way. I think this is what true fear feels like. I know something is very wrong and that I am at the center of it, but what?

Then the scene changes.

Now I'm in an empty parking lot and it looks sort of familiar, but I can't quite place the area. There's a woman in a car and from a distance she looks like Elizabeth. Is it her? There's a man tugging at the car door, trying to pull her out by her hair. Her beautiful curly hair. It is her!

I run toward them. The closer I get, the more the man's appearance alters. He's blond and big and ugly. It's Sergei. I swing on him hard and knock him to the ground. As I kick him in the back, another man comes for me. I don't know his name, but I recognize his face.

"You want some too?" I antagonize him.

"Da."

The man pulls out a large switchblade, but little does he know I've had my share of knife fights. The key is to disarm your assailant quickly. I kick him easily in the kneecap and when he bowls over; I kick his wrist and the knife goes flying across the blacktop. Now the fight's a fair one and we go blow for blow for several minutes until I see her.

The head bitch has Elizabeth by the throat and is taking her away. I can see the fear in her eyes. She mouths the words *I love you* as the woman moves out of my line of vision.

And now I can't see her at all.

I wake up in a sweaty haze like I've done after a night of some seriously bad drugs, but as soon as my eyes regain focus the pain kicks in. There are thin tubes of mysterious liquids being intravenously fed to my veins and none of them are pain killers? What kind of shit hospital am I in?

The first thing I do is look for her, but she is not in this room, and that's how I know that things are far worse than I could ever imagine. Perhaps my nightmares and actual life are slowly morphing into some sort of twisted new reality.

I feel around for the corded button that is usually attached to hospital beds so I can call a nurse. I want to know where I am and how I got here. Ah, that's right, the Russian bitch is real, and she is the reason I'm laid up in here and why I need to leave.

I press the call button with my thumb over and over until a nurse who looks all of twenty-one finally enters the room.

"Hello, Mr. Masterson. Welcome back," she says brightly.

It's difficult for me to respond because my throat feels unusually tight and constricted.

"Here let me help you sit up."

"My family," I try saying.

The nurse either cannot hear me or is ignoring my plea as she adjusts the height of the bed and fluffs the pillows behind my back.

"There that should help. Now, how about a small sip of water?"

She picks up a Styrofoam cup filled with water that has my name written in ballpoint pen ink on it. She holds the straw to my lips and I take a long sip, hoping that it will soothe some of the rawness I feel. I need to ask her where Elizabeth is.

"There now, why don't you try speaking again so I can help you."

"My family," I say. "Where is my family?"

"I'm sorry, Mr. Masterson, but I only came on shift an hour ago. I have seen none of your visitors, but I'll ask someone at the desk if they've seen anyone. I'm sure someone was here earlier."

"My phone."

"I'll check. By the way, I'm Karen, your nurse for this shift. If you need anything else tonight, I'm your girl."

Karen rummages through a plastic bag filled with some of my belongings. The bloody clothes I was wearing are in the bag, but no phone. Damn, I forgot that the Russians have it and my identification, which leads me to my next question.

"How do you know my name?"

"It says it right here on your chart. Roman Masterson."

"Yes, but how do you know that?" I cough. "Who brought me here?"

"I'll check with the desk. Give me a sec."

When Karen returns, she lets me know that it was Camden who brought and registered me to the emergency room, but that was over eight hours ago. I've been in this hospital for eight hours and Elizabeth still isn't here? Did that scumbag Sergei get his hands on her? Shit, I've got to get out of here.

I try moving, but my body feels like a wet bag of cement. It's a struggle to move any of my limbs.

Fuckkkk!

One of the monitors connected to me beeps faster and louder than before. Karen rushes back inside my room.

"Your blood pressure is going up, Mr. Masterson." She places her hand on one of my shoulders. "Please calm down and stop moving around so much."

I want to tell her to fuck off, but I can tell it would be wasted on Suzy sunshine.

"Are you in pain? I can increase the morphine drip if we need to."

I shake my head no as I try to calm myself. The last thing I need is to be comatose while I figure out how I'm going to get my ass out of this bed and get to my family.

"Oh, I almost forgot, the previous shift left a sticky note on your chart. The directions were to give it to you once you woke up."

The note simply reads: *I got you. -Cam*

An unfamiliar emotion fills my chest and clouds my head. I am so frustrated that I could cry, and I don't think I've really cried since I first found my mother passed out in our apartment and thought she was dead. I feel utterly helpless.

I am furious at Camden for leaving me in a hospital alone with no word about my family except for the cryptic-ass sticky note he left. I love that boy like a brother, but the next time I see him, I'm kicking his ass.

"I'll be right back, Mr. Masterson."

Karen returns with a fresh bag of liquid to attach to my IV. I try lifting my arm to stop hers but it won't cooperate so I just stare menacingly at her instead. The little girl doesn't even flinch. In fact, I almost think she thinks this is foreplay. She can't keep her eyes off of my ink.

"Don't worry, Mr. Masterson." She grins. "I'm just

replenishing your fluids and giving you a little some-thing to calm you down so you can rest."

"*I don't want to rest!*" I scream inside of my head, but whatever poison she injects into my veins works its magic and weighs heavily on my eyelids until they both shut completely.

I have no choice but to allow myself to drift off into a state of medicated unrest. The only thing I can hope for is that I'll see Elizabeth and Knox in my dreams.

19

ROMAN

"Where are they?"

As soon as my eyes open again the first thing I do is search for Elizabeth and Knox. Sadly, they're not here, but my assistant Jade is. Her small body is crouched like a tiger in a hospital room chair, not paying me any attention, wearing a crooked smile as she texts someone.

"They're not here yet," she responds while still typing on her phone.

"Why?"

I try turning on my side so she'll look at me.

"Stop panicking or I'll have Nurse Ratched turn up the morphine drip," she warns.

"I don't panic."

"I guess your voice feels better. The doctor said you were having trouble talking, but you seem to have plenty to say now."

I didn't even notice, but she's right. My throat feels a lot better. How long have I been asleep?

"How far away are they?" I ask. "Because the Russians—"

"Stop." She holds her hand up. "Last time your beloved checked in with me, which was like five minutes ago"—Jade rolls her eyes for dramatic effect—"she was about an hour from the station."

"You talked to her?"

"Yes, she's fine. She, Knox, and Juliette are on an express train bound for Thirtieth Street station. We didn't send a car because the train is faster and there're no planes flying out of *bumblefuck-wherever-she-is* Pennsylvania."

"Call her right now."

"No, you're just going to make her cry all over again."

"She was crying?" My stomach rolls from hearing that news.

"Her baby's daddy basically flatlined on the operating table, so yeah, she was bawling."

"I died?"

"Pretty much."

"And you told her that shit?"

"She's damn near your wife, so yes, I told her."

Fuck me.

"And who's handling—"

Jade holds her hand up to stop me from asking any more questions.

"You're not running the show right now. You fucked around and got yourself shot, so now the rest of the grown-ups are in charge."

I'm not in the mood for Jade's snark. This is a serious situation.

"Listen, you little chicken nugget—"

"Uh, uh, uh." She wags her finger at me. "I'm not the one who got tased and abducted from in front of his own neighborhood supermarket. I mean, how did you let that shit happen, anyway?" She laughs at me. "That's some amateur shit."

"Where's Camden?" I ask, ignoring her dig. It's enough that I'm going to be kicking myself in the ass for that mistake for the rest of my life. I don't need to hear it from her. I got too comfortable. Too soft as

Joseph would say. I will never make the same mistake again.

"He's taking care of a few out-of-town guests."

"They're still alive?"

"Three breathing Russians are still on the menu," she answers casually.

"Call him now, Jade. As long as they're still breathing Elizabeth and Knox are in danger." I grimace from a shooting pain in my stomach. "Fuck, did those quack doctors leave the slug inside me?"

"Hello?" Jade mockingly raps her knuckles on the bedside table. "Roman, are you there? You can't even take a shit by yourself right now and you want in on the Russians? Not happening."

"Help me get out of this bed."

"Nope, I've been ordered to keep you in the hospital and quiet by any means necessary."

"I pay you an ungodly sum of money to do whatever I tell you to do. Now get me my pants."

"Now get me my pants," she mimics me with a contorted look on her face.

"You're such a bitch sometimes."

"Actually, I'm a bitch all of the time but that's why you hired me."

"Did you at least take care of my phone and ID. They've got all my real shit."

"We were able to salvage your wallet with your ID from the warehouse, but I'm afraid your phone took a bullet straight in the eye."

All this talk of bullets is making my eye twitch.

"I need to talk to Cam."

"Can't do that," she singsongs.

"Do you remember when I generously offered you this gig? I specifically told you that you'd work for *all* of us, not just your favorite."

"Do you have a concussion too? Camden King is hardly my favorite!"

I flinch from a spasm near my broken ribs as I try to stop myself from laughing.

Jade is full of shit.

She has no clue what's coming for her. Cam's going to spin her head around ten times before she realizes what's happening, and I hope I'm lucky enough to have a front-row seat when it happens. How can someone this smart be so clueless when it comes to men?

She continues to crack a wad of gum she's been chewing on, trying to act like a hard-ass, but I know her. The little spitfire has probably been in this hospital since they wheeled me in here, giving the nurses and doctors hell all day and night worrying about my care.

"Oh, look at this." Her phone flashes. "You're in luck. It's the king himself."

Jade jumps from the chair, standing by my bed, and holds her cell to my head.

"I can hold it," I argue, not wanting to be treated like an invalid.

She pulls the phone back.

"You want to talk to him or not?"

"When Elizabeth gets here, I'm going to sic her on you for treating me like this."

"Ooh, I'm shaking in my boots."

Jade returns the cell back to my face.

"King." I greet him by one of my many nicknames for him.

"Rome. You good in there? Heard you might have seen the white light at the end of the tunnel last night."

Damn, does everybody know I almost died?

"Other than I feel like I've been run over by a Mack truck, I'm good. I guess God wasn't ready for me yet."

"I guess not, homie. Did Jade tell you Elizabeth and Knox are safe?"

"They aren't safe until I've got eyes on them."

"Understood."

"So are they Bratva?" I get straight to the point of this call.

"They're from the Popov family in Maryland. The woman's name is Irina and she is from the bloodline. Her son isn't in the family business because he's an idiot. They set him up out here with a few rentals to keep him out of the way, but Philly Bratva keeps an eye out to make sure he doesn't get into any real trouble."

"How did they know how to find me?"

"They frightened the girl. They threatened to kill her family in Utah and roughed her up a little, but she's okay. She didn't tell them much. But enough that they were able to put a tail on you. We put the girl on a plane back to Oregon, but to her credit, she tried to warn Elizabeth that the Russians were coming for you yesterday, but I guess she didn't get the message."

I don't give a damn about some sort of missed warning. All I care about now is that Elizabeth and Knox are safe and stay safe. I will regret for the rest of my miserable life if something happens to them because of my missteps, especially because of how angry Elizabeth and I were with each other when she left. I said goodbye to my boy, but I should have never let her get on that train without telling her that I loved her. I will never do that shit again. I've learned my lesson.

"I promised that bitch a reckoning for shooting me and threatening my family. Just keep her on ice for me. I'm going to handle her personally when I get out of here."

There is an awkward silence between us for a moment and the hair on the back of my arms rise.

"What aren't you saying, King?" There haven't been any lies between me and Camden since we were teenagers and he better not start now. "Spit it out."

"I don't have them yet."

"What do you mean?" I look at Jade as I continue talking. "Jade said they're alive."

"Cutter went a little overboard with the bomb and because of the amount of smoke we couldn't see that well. So they're alive, but I don't know where just yet."

Jade lowers her eyes as if she can run from the fact that she didn't tell me quite everything.

"So the three of you came in that warehouse like McGyver with homemade bombs and shit and didn't nail one of them!" I exclaim.

"Stop yelling," Jade chastises. "You're going to hurt yourself."

"The mission was to get *you* out of there, Rome, so it wasn't a total loss."

"We need to finish this. She will not stop coming for what's mine because I manhandled her precious little boy. I saw it in her eyes, Cam."

"I know this is easy for me to say but don't worry. I've got a lead on one of them, and where I find one, I will find the others. I always do. Plus, if it makes you feel any better, I'll even include the old man on the search and you know how I feel about him."

"Cam, don't fuck this up. You owe me."

"When have I ever fucked up a fix? And let's not forget that it was my tracker that saved your life last night. If anything, you owe me one."

"My hand is tired," Jade deadpans. "Can you two wrap this up?"

"Well, hand over the phone then," I tell her. "We're not done talking."

"Sorry, dude, but you're done. My phone needs charging."

She steps away from my bedside and says something I can't discern to Camden. I'm about to curse her out something awful when she walks back over to my bed smirking.

"Your beloved will be here in fifteen minutes, but

if you don't behave I'll tell them not to let her in the ICU."

"I'll have them kick your ass out instead."

"That's where you're wrong. Elizabeth is not your wife yet, so she has just about as much say in this place as I do. The difference between us is I've been here since you were rolled inside half-dead on a gurney, so I'd say the nurses who I bought a nice hoagie platter by the way are not going to throw me out—ever."

"You're fired."

Jade laughs. "No one else could stomach working for you and you know it, so I'll just chalk that up to the painkillers talking."

Then we're interrupted by a knock at the door.

20

CAMDEN KING

There is an unfinished basement underneath Club Lotus that is too humid and moldy for storage but great for interrogation. There are no windows and there is only one door which is bolted on one side.

I've successfully tracked down and have been hosting Roman's Russian guests down here while working on their final arrangements. No one knows they're down here besides me and my brothers because Jade probably wouldn't be able to keep it a secret from Roman, and that crazy fucker would figure out a way to roll his half-dead body out of bed and put a bullet in each of their heads.

While that would be a satisfying solution to end this story, the Bratva is a bitch to deal with when you decide to murder someone in their family, so it's probably best that we handle this another way.

With the help of my brothers, I've taken the prints of Irina's son and planted them in the dead girl's apartment from our fix in Chicago. I've also switched out Whitfield's prints for the son's in the Chicago PD's evidence database, and made the son look like a passenger on a flight to Chicago a day before the murder.

With a little help from Joseph, we hope that the department will avoid an investigation into their "fingerprint mistake" as long as there are some prints in the system that are linked to the case. It was completely wiping all prints from the case that was the problem. Hopefully, I've fixed that with the plant.

Heads will roll in the department and someone will lose their job for arresting the wrong person, but the bottom line is that they must allow our client to return to Miami and we would have done our job and get paid by Kat.

"So you see, Irina, I've arranged it so that there is a very long digital trail linking your son to a young girl's murder in Chicago. There will be no doubt that your son was there at the time and place of the killing, and he will go to prison for a very long time."

"What do you want from me?" she asks, looking like she's aged several years after hearing my revelation.

"This could have been a lot easier if you had pursued this whole matter with some civility. Do you just go around kidnapping people you don't know all the time?"

"I didn't know who Mr. Masterson was at the time."

"But you know now?"

"I'm starting to understand, yes."

"Then let me explain even further. You've made such a huge mistake that Ivan is not even coming for you. No family within two-hundred square miles of this place is going to help you."

Ivan is the head of the largest Bratva family in Philadelphia. He and Joseph have a long-standing relationship that dates back at least twenty years. Ivan owes the old man a favor and has agreed to turn a blind eye to this matter since it's personal and not Bratva business.

"You talked to Ivan?"

She swallows thickly and starts to look a tinge

green. She's worried because I know who Ivan is and seems to be truly starting to feel the weight of her miscalculation which gives me a feeling of satisfaction although I can't probably say the same for Roman. I'm not the one who got shot twice and kicked in the ribs.

"Do you want to know what he said?"

"How do I know that you truly spoke to him?"

"He said you'd say that, so I'm supposed to remind you of Paris in 2005."

Her face drops.

I do not understand what that date or place means to her, but it seems to satisfy her need for validation and she suddenly becomes more cooperative.

"What do you need me to do so that my son doesn't go down for these bogus charges?"

"Your son will not go free."

"What?"

"Your son terrified a young woman who means something to a friend of mine. He has to pay for that."

"If he goes to jail, then why must I negotiate with you?"

"Well, first, you should negotiate for your own self-preservation and second, I could arrange it so that your son never leaves prison for the rest of his miserable life. It's easier to do than you think. His appeals will get lost, his parole will get pushed back, and then next thing you know, nobody cares anymore and he's forgotten."

"What do you want, *mudak*?"

"First, I'd prefer it if you'd avoid calling me a Russian asshole or bitch or whatever the hell you just said."

"You keep a woman like me in a disgusting basement then you're a *mudak*."

"I fed you a nice chicken dinner."

"In a basement and it was cold."

Whatever.

"Next, we want a piece of your business as payment for the pain and suffering you've inflicted on my partner. He will have to spend some time recuperating, which is time away from our business."

"How much?"

"Twenty-five percent."

"I cannot give you twenty-five percent of Bratva business!"

"Twenty-five percent of *your* profits not Bratva. No one will ever know that you're giving a quarter of your money to us unless you tell them."

"Thieves." She spits close to my feet.

"Partners."

"I'm not giving a quarter of my business to you mutts."

I ignore her tirade. She will do exactly as she's told or she'll find herself six feet under.

"Finally, you will put these two lowlifes out of their misery. They're not important enough for me to have their blood on my hands, but they've got to go."

Her two enforcers start speaking rapidly in their native tongue. Probably begging for their lives. One of them even puts his hands in a prayer formation, but the woman shakes her head.

"I'll let you three say your goodbyes. The weapon is taped behind the pipe of that sink."

She raises an eyebrow, probably surprised that I'm allowing her access to a firearm but there's a method to my madness. I know what I'm doing. I return to my office upstairs where we watch the three of them from the camera monitors we had installed about a year ago.

"There's no way she's going to do it, Camden," Stone says. "I don't think the old woman is a cold-blooded killer of her own people."

"You better hope she doesn't do it," Cutter says.

"Roman wanted to deal with them himself and I've got to agree that he has every right after what they did."

"Roman almost died from that slug to his gut. He will not be on his feet for a while and we can't keep them down here indefinitely," I tell them.

"Did you ask Joseph about it?"

"I did."

"Okkkkay then," Cutter replies unconvinced of the soundness of this plan. "If you're sure."

"I'm sure."

While Irina's two enforcers' hands and feet are bound in front of them, we've allowed her to have some freedom around the basement. She searches for the weapon and says something to them in Russian once she locates it. They both frantically shake their heads no until she raises her voice at them.

My assumption is that they are begging for their lives, but that isn't it the case. She hands the one on Roman's shit list—Sergei—the weapon and sits on the bed. After smoothing her hair and placing her hands in her lap, she gives the directive.

"What the hell are they doing?" I wonder.

Sergei points and aims the gun at point-blank range to Irina's head.

"Oh, fuck!" Cutter exclaims.

I'm pretty stunned myself. This wasn't how this was supposed to go.

"Maybe that wasn't a good idea," Stone says to me. "Now their boss is dead and those two maniacs have a gun. How are we going to go back down there without getting our heads blown off?"

"Let's just watch," I assure my brothers, but I'm not truly sure of anything.

The two men have another heated conversation in Russian. They argue with each other over Irina's dead body until the arguing abruptly stops. Sergei shoots the other man, whose name I could never find, in the head.

Now there's just Sergei.

He sits on the floor and bends his head into the nose of the gun. When he pulls the trigger, nothing happens, and he slumps over in defeat.

"What just happened?" Cutter asks like he just watched a horror flick.

"I only put two in the chamber."

"Purposely?"

"I knew that whoever remained alive was going to take the fall for killing the other two. If she had killed them both like I told her to it would have been Irina which was the ideal outcome. I'd made us a sweet deal for us to get a good chunk of her profits, and I thought she'd do anything to save her son. But plans change, so now we deal with who we've got left–Sergei."

"Yo, Cam, you're a diabolical motherfucker and I mean that in the most respectful way, brother."

Cutter grabs me around the neck and kisses my head.

"The favor Joseph pulled with Ivan was only going to get us so far," I explain further. "We needed insurance that we wouldn't get any blow-back from this. The Russians need to believe that they did this to each other and for that we needed a fall guy."

"You think Rome will be okay with us allowing this one to still breathe?" Stone asks. "Isn't this the one he's got the hard-on for?"

"He won't be breathing very long," I assure them both. "This dude is low on the totem pole. One of the Russian families will take care of him to tie up loose ends and if we're lucky, maybe even Ivan will do it."

"Well, either way, one of us has to break the news to Rome."

"And one of us has to deal with the bodies."

"Ugh, I hate clean up. Can't we hire someone?"

"You know we can't. No one can link this back to the club or us. Even a cleaner."

All three of us look at each other, waiting for the other to step up. None of us do, so Cutter comes up with an alternative solution.

"Rock, paper, scissors?"

"Fuck it, let's do it."

"One, two, three shoot!"

All three of us simultaneously place a hand forward.

All scissors.

Damn, this may take a while.

21

ROMAN

"Is it okay for us to come in?" I hear Juliette cautiously ask Jade at the door.

"Yeah, he's awake. Come on in."

Then suddenly I'm assaulted by a mound of curls and soft jasmine scented curves. The pain is agonizing as Elizabeth showers my face with kisses, paying special attention to the scar on my face, oblivious that she may be injuring the new ones.

It doesn't matter though.

I'm happy as fuck to see her.

I tighten my eyes shut and thank whatever higher power is looking out for me and my family. Then I wrap the hand without tubes going into my veins into the base of her skull, gripping her hair as tightly as I can, considering the pain I'm in, and pull her in for a much-needed kiss.

"I'm so glad you're okay," she murmurs after we break. "I can't even imagine if I had lost you. If *we* had lost you."

Our foreheads touch as our eyes meld into each other. Everyone's attention in the room is on us but it doesn't matter because all I can feel is a sense of relief blanketing my bones. My girl and my son are safe and they are right here with me. I will never let them go again.

"What took you so long to get here, baby?"

"I came as fast as I could."

Her eyes well up again as she beams at me.

"Thank God," Jade interjects. "We were going to have to put him down like a grizzly bear if you two didn't come soon."

Juliette and Joseph saunter in with Knox in tow and then bring him over to my bedside. Joseph gives me a slight head nod and I know exactly what he's saying with no words being said. He's relieved to see I'm alive and well.

"Say hi to Daddy, peanut," Elizabeth coaxes Knox as she takes him from Juliette's arms. Tears streaming down her face.

Knox babbles several of his usual garbled words with great inflection at the end as to make his point. We both start laughing at what sounds like one of the most beautiful sounds I took for granted.

I kiss Knox on his forehead and run my hand down Elizabeth's face.

"When did you become such a crybaby?" I ask her smiling.

"I've always been one."

"Bitsy, give Knox to me. Joseph and I are going to go to the cafeteria for a second and we'll take him with us. Jade, you want to join?"

Jade pops her head up from her phone and looks at Juliette like a deer caught in the headlights.

"You mean me?"

"Yes, dear. You want to grab some snacks? I know you've been here holding down the fort for a long time. You must be famished."

I love my stepmother, but she's as obvious as a heart attack.

"Um, okay. They usually serve crap in hospital cafeterias, but I guess I can scrape something together at the salad bar."

"Alone at last," I say when the door shuts behind them.

Elizabeth gently traces the scar on my face with

her fingertips.

"At last."

"Did you get the deal done with Cabot?"

"That doesn't matter right now."

"It does to me."

Elizabeth stares at me in a way that she hasn't in a long time. As if I'm the most amazing man on the planet.

"I was too terrified about condition to discuss any business after I heard about what happened to you, but if you must know, he emailed me when I was on the train. The legal department will be sending me something this week or the next."

"Told you it was a done deal."

"You were right." She twinkles. "You're always right."

"Baby, until I've dealt with the people that did this to me I want you and Knox to go stay with Joseph and Juliette."

"Uh-uh, I'm staying right here."

"Why can't you ever listen?" I wince from either my broken ribs or the two bullet holes in my body. I'm not sure which. "What happened to the girl who trusted that I'd always do what's best for her? The woman who knows I'm always right."

"Her fiancé got abducted and shot twice because

of a favor he did for *her* friend, so now she's going to follow wherever her heart leads her and right now that's here in Mercy Hospital, Room 4708. They can set up a cot for me right here."

"They're not just going to let an eight-month-old baby sleep in here. That has to be breaking all sorts of safety protocol."

"Knox can stay with Joseph and Juliette."

"How's that going to work?"

"Juliette is going to help me transition him to a gentle formula for supplemental feedings. She's also going to give him a little more solid food midday. That should help reduce the frequency of the bottle feedings. He'll be safe there with them, right?"

I'm fucking shook.

Elizabeth has done a complete one-eighty.

Maybe there is a silver lining to this whole debacle.

"Yes, Joseph will protect him with his life if it ever came to that."

"Then we're good," she chirps. "But there's one more thing," she adds.

"Yes, baby?"

"I thought about keeping this from you at first but I don't want there to be any secrets between us."

"Agreed."

"So here."

Elizabeth pulls up a chair as close to the bed as she can then shows me an email on the screen of her phone.

Dear Elizabeth,

You were once kind to me in college which is why I'm writing. I tried calling you months ago to tell you this before your husband was attacked but I didn't get through. I'm hoping that it's better late than never to make this confession.

I didn't know it at the time when we were students studying in the computer lab at Penn, but you were dating a boy I've known since I was a little girl. Although I grew up across the country from him, his mom and my mom are best friends and have been since childhood. The boy's name is Ethan.

His family has not heard from him in over a year and they are convinced that his disappearance has something to do with you. Because of his complicated history, and lack of any evidence, the police aren't taking his missing person's case seriously. So I was asked to befriend you by my parents in an effort to find out any information I could and give them a lead.

I used the fact that my creepy landlord was harassing me as my "in" but didn't anticipate the avalanche of violence that would occur after your husband confronted him. In my defense, I didn't think you would send Roman to speak to him and I didn't know my landlord had ties to the Russian mafia until they came to my apartment to threaten me.

At first I wasn't going to tell you any of this, because maybe you did have something to do with Ethan leaving town, and maybe you and your husband are getting exactly what you deserved. But then I reconsidered. I hope you can forgive my part in what's happened, but I also hope that if you know anything about Ethan that you'll share it with the authorities.

Sincerely,
Patty

"Will I ever get rid of that asshole? I thought I was finally done hearing his name."

"Me too."

"Don't tell her shit about Ethan, Elizabeth. She thinks he was some sort of saint and you're what–his downfall?"

"There's nothing to tell. I don't know anything, remember?"

"And Cam put this ungrateful wench on a first-class flight to Oregon."

"I know and I'm sorry."

"You realize, me getting shot wasn't your fault, right?"

"I'm the one who asked you to help with Patricia and look what happened. You almost died because of someone with an agenda involving me."

"No, Duchess, you're wrong." I try to hide my flinching from her but it's hard. I'm in a great deal of pain. "Her vendetta is against me. I'm the one who made Ethan disappear and as far as the landlord, I was arrogant and didn't do my homework before I approached him, but trust me when I say that will never happen again. I promise you that."

Elizabeth deletes Patricia's phone number and then places her phone face down on the bedside table.

"Well, it's over. Right now I just want you to please use that call button and tell the nurse who no doubt is drooling over you everyday that you need some more pain meds. I can hear the agony in your voice. Then I'll set up my laptop on this table and we'll watch a movie until you fall asleep.

I don't know if you realize it or not but it's date night."

"No." I smirk. "I didn't realize."

"And when you wake up, Roman, I will be here," she says glassy-eyed. "I'll always be here."

She slides her hand into one of mine and I lightly clasp it. Tears the size of raindrops slide down her cheeks.

"Are you crying again, nerd?"

"This has been the craziest few weeks of my life. I'm emotional, okay?"

"Get in bed with me." I pat the side of the bed. "I'll calm your pretty little ass down."

"Now, you know there's not enough room for the both of us," She chuckles as she wipes her tears away. "And there's nothing you can do for me right now but get better and come home."

"I love you, Elizabeth." I kiss the back of her hand. "I love you and Knox so fucking much that it frightens me that I could have lost you both. It hurts like hell that I can't get out of this bed and show you how much properly."

She bends down and kisses me gently on the lips.

"You've already shown me properly, Masterson" she says into my mouth. "You lived."

22

ELIZABETH

I am keenly aware that Roman is nervous about this visit. As we sit in the back seat of a town car that Jade arranged to pick us up from the airport, I feel the frenetic energy of his left knee bouncing. I slip my hand into his massive one as I continue to look out the window of the car. He gives it a light squeeze to acknowledge the gesture and his knee suddenly stops moving.

Vegas looks and feels exactly like what I thought it would. People are ready to gamble, party and drink the moment they set foot in the city's limits. The airport lobby is filled with colorful slot machines, the streets are packed with casinos with brightly lit neon signs promising visitors the payout of their dreams, and there are tourists from all over the world who bring a certain unique vitality to the town.

"How many times have you been here?" I ask Roman. "I can't remember if you told me."

"Just about four or five."

"To gamble?"

"Yeah, something like that."

I decide not to ask any more questions about that because his answer leads me to believe that he was here for work or with a woman from his past, and I don't really need to hear the details about either of those.

"What's your favorite game?" I ask him.

"I prefer the private poker tables if I'm going to play at all."

"That's where the big rollers play, right?"

"Elizabeth, I appreciate the small talk, but it's unnecessary."

"What do you mean?"

"I know that you're trying to keep things light but the reality is that we're on our way to see a woman who has had very little to do with me for a very long time, and it's not going to be an easy reunion regardless of what you're hoping for."

"I'm not saying it's going to be all kisses and hugs but it doesn't have to be difficult either."

"But it will be."

"Why do you say that?"

I wish Roman would go into this with an open mind. I read a lot of parenting books during my pregnancy and they all suggested that new parents should try working on their our own "parental baggage" so we don't repeat the same patterns. I feel like my relationship drastically improved with my own parents when my father and Aunt Juliette reconciled, so I'm just hoping to get similar results for Roman and his mom.

"My mother was an addict for most of her adult life, so you don't think it's odd that she lives in a city notorious for its vices? I'm telling you now. You should be prepared for the fact that you're going to be deeply disappointed. She is probably living in a rinky-dink apartment, spending most of her money on her bad habits."

"I think you're the one who may be pleasantly surprised. When I spoke to her a few weeks ago she sounded good and is looking forward to seeing you again."

"Uh-huh."

As the driver continues past the city limits, Roman's body stiffens as the view transforms.

"Are you sure we're in the right neighborhood?" Roman leans forward to ask the driver.

"Whitney Ranch, right?"

"Yes," I respond.

"Then we're in the right place. Just another five minutes and we'll be at your destination."

We pull up to a relatively large Mediterranean home with an attached garage, pristine terra cotta roof, and an immaculately maintained succulent and stone garden in front. The house is drop-dead gorgeous and doesn't look like a place where the woman I've heard about would live.

Now I'm the one nervous.

A relatively minute man with a round pot belly answers the door. He's wearing a crisp white T-shirt and a pair of Bermuda shorts and pool slippers. This must be the man that Roman's mother mentioned in her apology letter to him.

He looks friendly as we approach the door.

"You must be Roman. I'm Peter."

He extends his hand forward. Roman pauses for a moment, but then finally accepts the gesture and shakes his hand as well.

"This is my fiancée, Elizabeth."

"Pleased to meet you, Elizabeth. Come on in, you two. Frances is in the kitchen preparing a couple of things. Hope you're hungry."

Peter leads us through the foyer to a beautiful great room and then farther through the house into the prettiest, airiest kitchen I think I've ever seen. The walls are a pale peach and every small appliance has its rightful place on the countertops. There's a wall of sliding glass doors that Peter walks us through that leads us to a second kitchen. This one is an impressive outdoor one complete with a built-in fireplace, stone grill, countertop with sink, and upscale wicker furniture.

I am duly impressed.

"They're here, Frances."

A tall woman with olive skin and a simple white sundress turns away from the counter holding a tomato and a paring knife. She's stunning and Roman favors her in almost every way, especially the eyes. If this woman was an addict for most of her life it hasn't seemed to have ravaged her beauty at all.

"Hi, Roman."

"Hi."

"You look... well." Roman's mother gives me a quick once-over. "And your Elizabeth is beautiful."

Roman nods silently.

"Thank you," I offer in return for the compliment.

"Did you leave the baby back in Philly?" she asks.

"Yes, he's spending some time with my aunt."

"And Joseph," Roman adds.

His mother blinks her eyes a few times as if she's stuck on how to respond. I think Roman's comment about Joseph being in our son's life may have hurt her. These are unchartered waters for us all and I imagine that his head is swimming with questions and feelings that he has been contemplating expressing to Frances for years but this isn't really the time to say them though. This is supposed to be an initial meeting, so he isn't speaking to his mother for the first time on our wedding day.

"That's fine. We'll meet him another time," she finally responds.

"Yep, we'll definitely figure it out," I say.

"So, I made a rather large taco salad and I'm grilling some skirt steak for dinner. Do you two eat meat?"

"Yes," I answer brightly for the both of us. "That sounds delicious."

"We weren't sure if you guys do dogs," Peter adds. "So we put Bonsai in the den. Would you mind if I let her out for a second? She probably needs to pee."

"Oh, we love dogs," I say. "You need not confine her on our account."

Roman is strangely quiet as Bonsai comes out to greet us. She's a spunky terrier mutt with soulful eyes and a friendly disposition. She takes a liking to my handbag and keeps trying to sniff inside of it.

"No, Bonsai!" Peter reprimands her.

"Oh, it's fine. She must smell our dog," I say to let them know it's all right. "The name Bonsai fits her. She's so cute."

"Can we get you a drink or something?" his mother asks. "Dinner will be ready in five minutes."

There's a flat screen on the stone wall above the fireplace which I continue to stare at in amazement. What do they do when it rains? We don't see outdoor spaces like this as much over on the East Coast because of the weather.

"I'll take anything with rum if you have it. I've stopped nursing recently and am excited to have cocktails any chance I get."

"Peter, can you grab the drinks please?"

"Coming right up," Peter says. "Rum for you, Roman?"

Roman isn't paying attention to any part of this conversation because he is busy watching the dog sprint around the yard.

"Juice for him. He's still taking pain medication for his injuries."

"You want me to put her away, Roman?" Peter asks, probably wondering if he's uncomfortable.

Roman bends down to scratch behind her ears, and Bonsai licks his hand.

"You told me I couldn't have a dog," Roman says in a sorrowful voice.

It's so quiet now that I think I just heard a hawk call from a mile away. I desperately wanted to keep this visit light and breezy, but I should have known... Roman does nothing light and breezy.

"You said you were allergic," he continues.

Frances places a plate of the grilled steak onto the large farmhouse-styled dining table then responds.

"Did I say that?"

"Yeah, you did."

"I probably didn't want to admit that we couldn't afford one," she says apologetically. "I'm sorry. I shouldn't have lied to you."

"Well, what were you spending all of Joseph's money on then?"

We haven't even had an appetizer and he's going straight for the jugular. It rocked him to the core to discover that he had been lied to his entire life by his mother. She lied to him for years, telling him that Joseph was his "dead-beat" biological father when that wasn't the truth at all. That kind of lie is not a simple thing to just get past. Your mother is the first woman you trust. If you learn that you can't depend on the person who gave you life, then how do you trust anybody?

An uneasy look conforms on Peter's face as he keeps his eyes trained on Roman. He is clearly very protective of Frances and doesn't like the direction of the conversation. Hell, I don't like it either, but this is a discussion that's overdue, and I will stand by my man to make sure he gets what he needs.

"I thought I explained things to you in the letter," she asserts.

"Yeah, but now I want you to tell me to my face."

"Wait a minute now," Peter interjects uncomfortably.

"No, Peter. It's fine," his mom says. "Roman, I spent the money to get high. I spent any money we had to get high. Is that the answer you were looking for?"

"And that's why I couldn't have a dog like this one?"

"Yes."

"Or a hot dinner?"

"Roman."

Okay, now I'm thinking I need to stop this conversation before it gets nasty.

"And now you have all of *this*?" He walks the length of their yard with his arms fully extended to show his point. "This shit is impressive, Ma."

I can definitely see his point. Roman had a tough childhood where for the longest time he felt alone and as if he wasn't wanted. Many of the boys in his old neighborhood might have had absentee fathers, but most of them at least had their mothers. He didn't. She was a ghost of herself and not really present. So that's probably a scar he will carry with him for a very long time, and personally, I believe Roman's mother needs to accept her responsibility for her part in that. A letter probably wasn't the best way to start.

"Real estate is not as expensive here as it is where you're from. Don't be fooled by what you see here. We're not rolling in it. We're just living life like regular folks," Peter says, although I don't think he's really helping.

"Not the right answer," Roman responds. "Sounds like a bunch of bullshit to me."

Frances washes her hands and wipes them with a tea towel. She walks over and stands in front of

Roman, staring him square in the eyes. Two sets of identical obsidian pupils taking inventory of each other. Two people hurting. Two people struggling to work through a painful past.

"I said it in the letter, but maybe I should have waited until I could have said it in person. I see now that it wasn't the right approach. I apologize to you, Roman. I was barely human when I was an addict. Drugs were all I cared about. I didn't deserve you and I wasn't fit to raise you, but by the miracle of God you came to be a good man just the same. And now, by his grace, you're getting married to the mother of your son and the love of your life. I'm so grateful for the man you've become."

She's working the hell out of her apology, I'll give her that. But she's going to have to continually work at it, because Roman wants assurances that she has truly changed her life before he allows her into ours, and I'm in full agreement with that. I'm under no grand illusions that we can tie this up in a nice tidy bow by the end of tonight. This is just the beginning.

I take full responsibility for the crummy idea of us getting married in Vegas and having her attend as our special guest, but that was me not thinking things through. A wedding should be considered and planned seriously, and only for the benefit of the couple saying the vows. It's not a tool for me to use to mend fences. It's not just some random date on the calendar where I'm going to dress up in a pretty gown and party with my friends and family. It's the day I will promise Roman in front of everyone who has ever meant anything to us that I will love him until our last dying breath.

That is some serious shit.

Which is why we reworked our bet. He agreed to fly here for a visit with Frances as long as I set a date for a wedding back home.

I did.

"I am sorry for the pain I must have caused you. You can't imagine all the regrets I carry with me, son," she continues. "There were days when I almost thought the damage I caused in my past was too much to bear, but that's when this wonderful man here saw something worth saving in me and has been by my side ever since."

"We can understand that sort of devotion. That's exactly how I feel about your son. He's been there for me at my lowest points but has only seen the best in me. Sometimes I have to pinch myself because of how lucky I was to have met him again."

Roman walks over and embraces me from behind, kissing the curve at the back of my neck.

"Damn lucky," he agrees.

He holds me close as he musters the courage to do what he never thought he could.

"I appreciate the apology, Ma."

"Thanks for flying all the way out here to hear it."

We all sit at the beautifully set table and dig into Frances's yummy looking taco salad and steak.

"Did you say that you were lucky to have met *again*?" Peter asks through a mouth full of food. "How do you two know each other? Frances didn't tell me much about how you met."

The both of us glance at each other and smile as we reply simultaneously.

"It's a long story."

23

ROMAN

"Are you ready to get married?"

Never in a million years did I think I would ever hear that question.

Not from Joseph.

Not from anyone.

I just knew it was my destiny to forever be popping bottles and sleeping with whatever flavor of the month was on the menu. Who knew that when I was tasked to protect the little nerd who moved into my house that over a year later I'd be putting on a suit, getting married, and Joseph would be my best man.

"Yeah, old man, I've been ready."

"Are you still set on wearing those boots with your tuxedo?"

"You know I always dress down my suits."

"On your wedding day?"

"Elizabeth likes it and that's all that matters," I reply as I straighten the tie I'm wearing with my custom-tailored black on black tux.

"Sentiment has made you soft."

"Maybe, but it's also made me happy as fuck."

Joseph nods with acceptance. "Good."

"Did you see Frances and Peter sitting out there?" I ask.

"Yeah, I saw them." He sounds unimpressed.

"Did you speak to her?"

"I was cordial, although I don't think her chubby little boyfriend likes me."

"Did you apologize to her for your part in keeping us apart all this time?"

"Hell no," he asserts. "I'd make the same choices all over again."

I chuckle to myself. I didn't really think he'd ever apologize. Sorry isn't really a part of Joseph's vocabulary.

"Knowing that Juliette would be furious with you?"

He grins like he knows some sort of secret. "Even then."

Then he adds, "Your mother seems like she's finally in a good place though, so I'm happy for her."

"She looks clean but I think I'm going to wait before we talk about exchanging Christmas gifts and shit."

"Understood. So, I suppose we need to have a talk before you walk down the aisle?"

"Don't you think we're a little past the whole birds and bees conversation?" I say mockingly as I check to make sure I don't have any traces of candy in my teeth. "I think the fact that your grandson is the ring bearer should be a sign that I've aced that lesson."

Joseph starts his monologue anyway. The older he gets, the more he likes to talk.

"People tell you that marriage is a partnership."

"Yep, that's what I've heard."

"Well, it ain't. Marriage is never fifty-fifty. Sometimes it's eighty-twenty. Sometimes its sixty-forty. But whatever the ratio, it will always be your job to protect your family at all costs, and that includes Elizabeth and Knox now. Do whatever you have to do to protect what's yours and you will always be able to rest your head at night knowing that you've done your job."

I stop primping myself and stare hard at my father.

"I think the topic of this speech is interesting considering that you were the one that put a bullet in that asshole Sergei's head. How am I supposed to rest my head now knowing that you did my job?"

"You missed the entire point of my story."

"Nah, I think I got it."

"Not if you're asking why it had to be me and not you who handled the Russian. You of all people know that I've worked my ass off, so I never have to get my hands dirty anymore, but like I said, a man can sleep at night knowing that he did everything humanly possible to protect what's his. You have been and will always be my son, Roman, so I needed to handle that threat personally. I couldn't trust anyone else to do it, even Ivan, so rest assured this entire incident has been put to rest."

Joseph walks over to the bar in my hotel suite and pours himself a lowball of whisky before I can even say anything in response. In all sincerity, I don't know what to say.

For years I worked as the muscle for Joseph in our business. I've done the dirty work even when it was hard. He has never once cut me any slack or given me a pass. I think the old man is getting softer with age, but you know what? I think I like it.

"You want one?" he offers. "Anxious about taking the vows?"

"Nah, old man. I've been waiting for this day for a long time. I'm calm as a cucumber."

"I can't believe that you won over Elizabeth's parents. That father of hers is a pain in the ass. He always has been."

"I wouldn't say they're completely won over, but we have an understanding."

"Which is?"

"They understand that if they want to see their grandson that they better be polite to his father."

"I guess Knox is a highly effective blackmailing tool." He chuckles. "It's the eyes."

I stand in front of Joseph and take a deep breath, then silently go for it. We'll probably be at odds with each other about something again one day, but not today. I wrap my arms around him and give him a tight bear hug. His body stiffens until I tell him what I probably should have said a long time ago. What perhaps every parent wants to hear from their children. What I hope to hear from Knox one day.

"Thanks for everything, Joseph."

The overpriced wedding planner that Juliette just had to hire for us knocks once and peeps her head into the room.

"Are you ready, Mr. Masterson? Are you feeling any wedding jitters?"

Why does everyone keep asking me that shit?

I've been ready to make Elizabeth mine in not just body and soul but on paper too. It's funny. I grew up believing that infamous lie boys tell girls about how there's no difference between living together and marriage. I think we tell each other that horseshit because we're young and dumb and we don't want to think any woman has the power to control us or hold us back from "better pussy."

Now that I'm older and wiser, I see the reality of things. Boys are indeed always worried about making a mistake or missing out on something, but grown-ass men know when they've got a good thing and if they're smart, they lock down their women as quickly as they can. It may have taken a bullet in the gut to propel Elizabeth into wedding mode, but whatever works, right?

She's mine.

"Ready."

"Great! I'll go check on Elizabeth then."

"What do you mean, check on her?" A minor panic settles in the back of my throat. "Is she okay?"

"The bride always takes a little longer than the groom. That's just par for the course. I'll get a hold of her."

I sit on the couch in my suite and lean forward with my head between my hands.

She'll get a hold of her?

"Ready for that lowball now?" Joseph smirks. "Told you, you were getting soft."

"Just be quiet and pour the whiskey, old man."

Our glasses clink.

"Cheers."

ELIZABETH

"How does it look out there?"

"Amazeballs," Sloan declares.

"Are the lights low and the candles lit?"

"Check!" my friend Tiny cheerfully affirms.

"Is all my family in place?"

"Yes, Knox is sitting happily on your mom's lap, Mr. Tibbs is at the front looking cute in his doggy tuxedo, and I think half the town of Penn-Washington is here."

"So then there's no reason for me to wait any longer."

"Not unless you want to Thelma and Louise this bitch and run away," Sloan says chuckling.

"Sloan!" Tiny exclaims.

"Never," I assure them. "I'm more sure about what I'm about to do than I have been about anything before."

"Then why haven't you been answering your phone for the last thirty minutes?"

"I just needed a technology free moment on my wedding day."

"Well, explain that to your Prince Charming, because he has left his suite at the Ritz and is driving at warp speed to get here. He's been texting both me and Tiny, very nasty messages by the way, to make sure you're okay."

It was my idea for Roman and I to sleep apart over the last three days. I'm at home with Knox and he's been staying at a hotel. We're such a non-traditional couple in so many ways, I wanted us to be traditional about at least a few things. He hates the idea, and I admit it may not be one of my better ones. Being apart makes us both anxious, especially after the shooting.

"Aww, he takes such good care of me."

"Take care of you? He's texting like a maniac because he's probably afraid you're going to run."

"Roman knows good and well that I'm not going anywhere."

"Well, now that you've gone and had his love child, you can't." Sloan laughs. "That ship has sailed."

I smooth the sides of my dress, which practically skims my every curve. It's a modern, sleek, silk, full-length halter styled gown with a simple tulle veil that ends at my chin.

"You look amazing, Bitsy," Tiny tells me.

I can't believe I was ever worried about how I was going to look with my extra weight in a wedding gown. The seamstress did an excellent job of making sure the dress skimmed my curves and didn't squish them in like a sausage.

"Yeah, girl, you make a stunning bride. The dark knight should consider himself the luckiest man alive today."

No, I'm the luckiest.

"Go get my dad," I tell my two maids of honor who are both dressed in strapless white cocktail dresses. "I'm ready."

Roman and I are having a black and white wedding in Club Lotus on a Friday night for obvious sentimental reasons. Friday, because that's our date night and the club because it's where we first met (well, sort of). It's a special place for us.

The club has been closed to the public for a week and magically transformed into an elegant room full of white lights with reams of sheer white fabric that hang from the ceiling beams and large white balloons clustered and weighted in specific areas of the room. We covered all the tables in white linen tablecloths with simple white candles of various heights in the center and there are enormous bouquets of sunflowers interspersed throughout the room which add a pop of color and are also a part of the running private joke between us.

Getting married in a non-religious venue has been a sore spot between my parents and I, but honestly I don't think any place else could rival the sublime beauty of this space. I think the wedding planner got exactly every detail right. The club looks like an elegant, ethereal, otherworldly place. A space befitting our union. It is non-traditional; it is unique, and it is all us.

The walk down the aisle, which is covered in golden sunflower petals, seems long and awkward as everyone's eyes in the room are on me. It's a bit unnerving to see almost everyone you've ever known stare at you with generous smiles and shiny eyes. As I continue down the aisle, I hear a few complimentary whispers from the crowd.

"You look beautiful, Elizabeth."

"That dress is stunning."

I stop at the front row where Knox is sitting in his baby tuxedo and I give him a quick peck on the lips. For a moment he reaches out his arms for me to pick him up, but then my mom redirects him with his favorite teething toy. Both he and I have come a long way. He's becoming slightly more independent and I'm allowing him to be.

My father holds me steady as we continue to slowly walk to the front where I am now focused on the only person in the room who matters at this moment.

Roman.

He literally takes my breath away, looking hotter than I've ever seen him in his custom-made monochrome black tuxedo with the shirt slightly open and new leather boots on instead of shoes. I love the way his suit contrasts against the ink peeping from under his collar and from under his cuffs. His deep, intense, inky eyes hold mine in place as my father literally hands me over to him.

Is it irreverent to say in the middle of my

wedding ceremony that I want to climb this man like a pole?

"Take care of her," my father says.

"Always," Roman assures him.

Roman clasps my hand and leans in to whisper in my ear before the officiant has time to start.

"I missed you like crazy."

"I did too."

"You look incredible."

"You look hot."

He smiles.

"I will make you happy, Duchess."

I squeeze his hand tighter.

"You already do."

My friend Zoe is not only a celebrated tattoo artist in the area, but she also is an ordained minister in the state of Pennsylvania (thanks to the Internet) and is officiating our wedding. The plan is that after the ceremony we'll get wedding ring tattoos inked by her while our guests are at the cocktail hour.

"I've had the pleasure of getting to know this couple for a while and I think we can all agree that they are a unique pair," Zoe begins.

The crowd nods and murmurs in agreement.

"So, I'm sure you're not surprised that the bride

and groom have decided to recite their own vows. Elizabeth, ladies first."

I was nervous about saying my own words in front of a room full of people, but I knew that it wouldn't be right to let this day go by without sharing with all the people who care about us why I have chosen to spend the rest of my life with this man.

Roman and I turn toward each other and hold hands. I stare deep into his eyes reminding me we are the only two people in this room, reminding me I have nothing to be frightened of or embarrassed about, and reminding me that with him by my side there is nothing I can't do.

I gingerly clear my throat.

"Today, I am the most blessed woman in the world. I am marrying my best friend, the father of my child, my protector, and my lover. I promise to take care of the heart you have given to me so willingly. I promise to honor and respect you for the rest of our days. I love you, Roman."

I cannot see Sloan or Tiny because they are standing behind me, but I can hear Sloan starting to sniffle. She promised me she wouldn't fall apart today because if she starts the waterworks then I'm bound to lose it.

I lower my head for a moment and breathe deeply through my nose and out my mouth to collect my composure when Roman takes a curved finger and raises my chin to meet his gaze.

"Elizabeth."

His baritone voice ripples right through me and goes straight to my tear ducts.

I think I'm the one who's going to lose it first.

25

ELIZABETH

"The fact that a guy like me is standing in this room with a woman like you on our wedding day astounds me. You are intelligent, brave, sexy, gracious, and a warrior. You see the best in everyone because you are truly the most genuinely real and kind-hearted person I have ever met. I promise to love you, respect you, cherish you, honor you, protect you, and make love to you all the days we have left on this earth."

The crowd giggles at his last part of the vow.

"You may now exchange rings."

Joseph hands Roman a box I didn't know about. I already have a beautiful diamond engagement ring that I love, but this is something different. It's a delicate gold ring made of gorgeous yellow and chocolate diamonds in the shape of a sunflower, and it matches the other beautiful jewelry he's given me to remind me of our beginnings. A bully and a naïve kid who were destined by familial ties and circumstances to meet again. More tears swell as I consider how much thought he put into this wedding gift.

I will not ruin my mascara.

God, this man is perfect.

Sloan steps forward and hands me my box for Roman. Although we are getting tattoos around our ring fingers to symbolize our forever bond, I wanted to make sure he had a traditional wedding band that he can wear whenever he chooses. There are three diamonds set deep in the band to represent the unification of him, me, and Knox as a family and there is a simple inscription inside memorializing today's date.

"Will you Roman Masterson take Elizabeth Hill to be your lawful wedded wife for richer or for poorer, in sickness and in health, till death do you part?"

"I do."

"And will you Elizabeth Hill take Roman Masterson to be your lawful wedded husband for richer or for poorer, in sickness and in health, till death do you part?"

"I do."

"By the power vested in me by the state of Pennsylvania, I now pronounce you husband and wife. Roman, you may kiss your bride."

Roman slides his arms around my waist and firmly pulls me into his embrace.

"Pleased to meet you, Mrs. Masterson."

His deep voice rumbles through my entire my body and lands at my core with passion and promise.

"Hi." I can't stop smiling.

The kiss to salute our union is chaste by our usual standards, but I still think it's wildly romantic. I taste a mixture of mint, whiskey, and chocolate on his tongue, which is uniquely him and tastes like home.

Our evening flies by in a flurry of hugging, dancing, and food in no particular order. Juliette warned me it would indeed fly by, and that I'd want to take a moment to pause and soak in everything around me: the atmosphere, the people, and the love around me because in a blink of an eye the night would be over. That's hard to do when you're in the middle of it, but

I have no doubts that I will remember this night forever. It was perfect.

I wouldn't have changed a thing.

Juliette arranged for the deejay to play a set of nineties radio hits, which turned out to be the highlight of the evening. Everyone including many of the older guests from my old neighborhood in Penn-Washington jumped up on the dance floor and were jamming to old TLC and Britney Spears songs. I even think I saw old Miss Dorothy breaking a sweat.

"Do you see Miss Dorothy over there trying to do the running man right now?" I say while dancing next to my mom.

"I didn't know her knees could move like that."

"Me either. I thought her knees were why she never pulls any weeds out front?"

"Yeah, I guess that's been her excuse for fifteen years."

We both roar with laughter.

"Everyone is having a good time, Bitsy. You and Roman throw a splendid party. I hope you're enjoying it."

"I am, Mom."

I truly am.

"Look at your father over there with Knox. Those two are becoming thick as thieves. Remember how he was afraid to hold him when he was first born? It was just a matter of time before Knox won him over. There's something absolutely magnetic about that boy. He's going to be a heartbreaker, just like his daddy."

"What do you mean by that?" I take offense, "Roman's no heartbreaker."

"Look at poor Trisha and Marie over there."

I glance over at a table of some of my younger cousins. Trisha and Marie are both fourteen years old and they're staring at Roman in the way that half of the female gender drools over Chris Hemsworth.

"Are they crushing on my husband?" I giggle.

"That they are."

I've danced half the night away and gorged myself on wedding cake when it's time for Roman to pull the garter down my leg and toss it into a sea of single men. The deejay plays some cheesy instrumental song as the crowd cheers when Roman gets on his knees in front of me.

I lick the corner of my lips as my sexy husband slowly inches his hand up my dress, and then blush knowing that there are people watching him basically seduce me in the middle of the dance floor. He maintains my modesty by holding my dress down as he reaches his hand farther and farther up to do something immodest. There's a crooked smile across his mouth as he brushes a few of his fingertips against the damp fabric of my silk thong. Once he has the garter in hand, he holds it high for the guests to see.

"Let me find out that you get turned on when people watch, Duchess," he practically growls in my ear.

One of the more touching moments of the evening is when the deejay calls for couples only on the dance floor. Since all of our babysitters are dancing, we decide to include Knox in on our dance together. All the favorite couples in our lives dance around us to "Marry You" by Bruno Mars, and Knox bounces up and down in Roman's arms between us.

His happiness is infectious, or maybe it's mine that is, because I dance joyfully to the music as I hold my dress up and twirl in my bare feet.

"You are the most beautiful woman in this room," he says loud enough for me to hear over the music.

"I should be. I'm the bride."

"What else do we have to do tonight, baby? We took the photos, we cut the cake, we threw the garter and flowers at our friends."

"Jade didn't look too thrilled that she caught the

bouquet. She ruined a perfectly good bunch of sunflowers."

"And Camden was a little ticked off that he *didn't* catch the garter. Your neighbor's son might need an escort out of the club tonight. I think Cam is going to kill him for sliding the garter up Jade's leg like that."

"That was kind of funny."

"I'm ready for it to be just the two of us, Duchess."

"Stop rushing this wonderful evening, husband."

"Say it again."

"Husband." I smile.

"Louder."

"Husband!"

Roman leans over for another kiss with the baby between us.

"Come here."

Knox babbles a string of words as he gently touches our chins with his small, sticky hands.

"I think he just said Dada!" Roman says excitedly.

"You're hearing things, baby. He can't talk yet."

Frances and Peter walk over to us with their eyes focused right on Knox. They haven't really had an opportunity to spend any time with him because we've both been too busy for another Las Vegas visit before the wedding.

"Would it be okay if I held him for a while?" Frances asks.

I give Roman a moment to answer his mother and when he stands there hesitating; I answer for him.

"Sure," I agree. "Here you go."

The deejay throws on a series of line dancing songs, one right after another, and Sloan and Tiny pull me away from my new husband to dance together.

"Sorry, dark knight, but the wobble is our song. Gotta go!"

As I party with my friends, Roman moves from table to table taking pictures and shaking hands. I watch him work the wedding guests with an ease and comfort I've never seen him exhibit before. He is genuinely happy and it feels good that I played a major part in putting that look on his face.

That in itself is worth every bit of pain that has brought us to this day.

This wonderful day.

26

ELIZABETH

It's my wedding night. A night I have contemplated many times this past year. I don't know exactly why I feel so incredibly nervous at this moment, but I do. Our love is battle worn and has been tested countless times, and I know without a doubt that man loves me with every fiber of his being, so that's not the issue. I have slept with Roman a bazillion times and we've done some raunchy stuff together (at least by my standards) so that's not the issue either.

I think the actual source of my trepidation is that I've put an enormous amount of pressure on myself to have the best sex of my life tonight because that's what you do on your wedding night, right? I wonder if Roman is feeling anything similar.

We leave our friends and family to enjoy the rest of the wedding reception and take a car to Penn's Landing where Roman's yacht is waiting. Our honeymoon plan is to take a two-week-long cruise alone down the East Coast making stops in Miami, The Bahamas, and Puerto Rico and then turn back around. I didn't plan any tours or activities for our time in the Caribbean. We're just going to veg out on the beaches and on the deck of this ship, although it will be a genuine challenge to my workaholic tendencies and his controlling ones.

We're greeted by the captain and a crew of staff that Roman hires when he makes plans to take the yacht out. Two staffers handle our luggage as another guides us to the top deck. The deck is elegantly decorated similarly to our reception space, with strings of white lights along the banisters, over-sized modern furniture with deep white cushions, and bouquets of sunflowers. Soft music plays from the speakers and there's a table full of mini-sized desserts.

"Congratulations, Mr. and Mrs. Masterson," the young woman offers. "Please make yourselves comfortable and call down if you need anything else this evening."

The staff scatters to do whatever it is they do on this oversized boat, and Roman and I are finally alone for the first time of the night.

Roman sits in one of the oversized round chaises, and I notice that he slightly winces as his butt hits the chair. While we are several months removed from his abduction, there are still plenty of scars that remain, including some chronic pain in his shoulder and torso that he continues to work on in physical therapy.

"Come sit next to me, Duchess."

He pulls me by the waist and plops me down next to him.

"Did you take any pain medicine today?" I ask.

"I was drinking, so I didn't want to mix the two."

"The drinking doesn't kill the pain though."

"I know what will kill the pain," he says suggestively.

"We just got on the boat and you're ready to ravage your wife already?"

"I'm always ready."

"I should've changed out of my dress before we came to the dock," I say, kicking off my heels.

"I love that dress. I want to fuck you in that dress."

"Roman." I blush.

He pulls my feet onto his lap and rubs them. Funny how you never know just how badly heels hurt until someone massages your feet. I feel like I've died and gone to heaven.

"Mmm, that feels great."

"That was an unforgettable night tonight, Duchess. Thank you for saying yes."

"As if there would have been any other answer."

"For a minute, it looked like you wanted us to live in sin forever."

Roman works his magical fingers up my tight calves.

"I lost my compass for a moment and almost losing you put everything back into perspective and back on course. You and Knox are what matters and everything else comes second."

"I ditto that," he says in a jagged voice.

His hands slowly push up my dress so it bunches at my hips.

"Roman," I say hesitantly, looking around the deck for any employees.

"Stop acting like you're self-conscious about being seen with your husband. I think you like people to watch. Remember when one hundred people were watching my hands up your dress an hour ago?"

"Oh, be quiet."

"It turned you on, Duchess. Admit it."

"It turned me on because your hand was at my crotch."

"Like it is right now?"

I bite my bottom lip as I worry that staff may be close by.

"No one is coming up here unless we call for them. Tonight, it's just Mr. and Mrs. Masterson sailing under the stars."

"I am Mrs. Masterson, aren't I?" I giggle proudly.

"Yes, the fuck you are."

Roman's hands are working several of the hook and eye closures of my bridal corset. Carefully unfastening each one until the garment is loose. He pulls it down my body from underneath the dress and slings it across the deck.

"You had to be suffocating in this."

I exhale in relief.

"It feels good to finally have it off," I admit.

Roman has long since taken off his jacket and tie, but now loosens some buttons of his shirt and kicks off his boots. He grabs my hand and we walk over to the side of the ship. I watch with marvel as the dark waves ripple underneath us as we pick up speed on the open water.

"What a beautiful night to have become your wife," I say.

He stands behind me as we lean by the railing, steadily inching up my dress as he softly kisses the curve of my neck.

"Spread your arms across the railing, Duchess. Feel the breeze as we move against the water."

He slides several of his fingers in between my legs, which are only covered by the smallest piece of white lace, and breathes heavily by my ear.

"I spent three long nights in a hotel bed waiting for this."

He slides a finger inside of me.

I moan from the intrusion.

I blew my hair out for the wedding and it falls down my back in smooth beach waves that actually took over an hour to create. Roman slides his hand to the base of my neck and tugs on my hair.

"Never deny me what's mine again," he growls. "Ever."

"No," I pant. "Never again."

"Good girl."

He pulls his finger out of me and releases my

hair, then unzips my dress. It falls to the ground and now I am standing in nothing but a wet wedding thong.

I don't need to turn around to hear him unbuckling himself, but decide to look anyway. I lean back on the railing, arms spread, nipples to the wind, and stare at my husband with wicked intent.

I am no longer nervous or skittish about what comes next because this beautiful man is my husband and I'm going to make love to him on *our* yacht on *our* wedding day naked as a jaybird and it will be perfect.

"I love you," I tell him as I slide off my thong and toss it back in the water. "Now come get what's yours."

Roman practically snarls as he turns me back around, bends me forward, and ruthlessly enters me from behind.

The intrusion is exquisite and my mouth hangs open as he repeatedly thrusts and pounds us both to a violent orgasm.

"Fuckkkk!"

"That mouth," he chides semi-seriously, "is getting out of hand, Duchess."

Roman completely strips out of all of his clothing, grabs one of the large cushions from the chair and tosses it on the ground.

"Get on all fours."

"I wonder if you realize that your reprimands are always rewards," I tease.

"Quiet," he says, as he strokes himself to full mast again.

I drop to the cushion and get on all fours. I watch as he studies me intently, then kneels on the cushion directly in front of me. I lick my lips as I stare directly at the head of his penis.

"Maybe this will keep you quiet."

He slides his dick inside of my hungry mouth and I work his length with the precision of an expert, opening my throat and swallowing him deep. He stares at me with deep love and admiration as I pleasure my husband in one of my favorite ways until he grabs me by the hair.

"Stop."

He bends down and kisses me hard.

I am sopping wet and need him inside of me desperately. My head is spinning. He keeps starting all of these delicious things and never letting us quite finish. It is making me want him that much more.

He stands and walks around behind me, then

starts playfully slapping my ass. He's been obsessed with it since I had the baby. It's wider and jiggles more, and he definitely really likes it.

"Spread your legs wider and raise your head and look at the water while I fuck you properly, wifey."

He enters me slowly this time. Pulling and pushing himself inside of me, inch by inch. When he's anchored himself all the way, he leans over, holding himself up with one hand and grabbing one of my breasts with the other. He squeezes my nipple as he rhythmically rams himself hard inside of my quivering pussy.

I yell in bliss with each powerful thrust he executes because I can. There's no sleeping Knox to worry about. I don't care about whatever people on this ship that can hear us. And fucking by the water makes me feel powerful, as if I'm some sort of intoxicating goddess.

It feels too damn good.

The beginnings of an orgasm bend and twist inside of me, and so do the tears. I'm overwhelmed with the emotions of the day and with the fact that I am about to explode. Blood rushes to my head as my entire body contracts from the release Roman extracts from me.

I slump to my stomach from exhaustion and

Roman lies next to me and starts playing with my hair. I turn over to face him and run my hand down the side of his face, still coming down off the high of our lovemaking.

"Can I tell you something?" I ask reservedly.

"It depends."

"On what?"

"If you tell me while I'm inside of you."

I smile and look between his legs and notice that he's growing hard again.

Unbelievable.

He smoothly glides his hand in between my legs to my swollen pussy and gently skims the top of my clit with his fingers, coaxing it back to neediness. I'm surprised how rapidly my climax is building again.

"Don't come," he whispers. "I want to be inside of you when you grip my dick like a vise."

He rolls on top of me, placing my legs over his shoulders for a twist on the missionary styled position. We haven't done this in a while because of the gunshot wound to his shoulder, and I'm not sure we should do it now. I don't want to aggravate his injury.

"Roman—"

"Shh," he quiets me. "I'm fine, baby."

He slides his semi-erect dick back inside and rocks into me slowly matching the motion of the boat. We stare ardently into each other's eyes as he moves deeply inside of me. My eyes almost roll to the back of my head as he grows harder and damn near hits my cervix.

"Now, say what you had to tell me," he says in between strokes.

"I love you."

"And I love you."

"And—"

He tilts to the side, fucking me from a different angle. It takes my breath away for a moment and I can't get my words together.

"You were saying?" He grins mischievously.

"I was saying—"

"Uh-huh?"

"Masterson," I plead.

He laughs sinisterly while I grab my breasts to keep them from hitting me in the damn eye as I absorb his deliciously punishing strokes.

"More," I demand because I'm almost there. "I'm so close."

"Greedy girl."

I can see that his next orgasm is coming for him too.

"Uh-huh, I'm greedy."

"Dirty fucking girl," he growls.

My orgasm won't be denied. It's coming hard and fast like a freight train and I arch my back from the intense pressure as he grunts his way through his.

"You're going to kill me," I say, completely out of breath.

He laughs out loud.

"That's the idea, baby, and just imagine, you have two weeks of this coming to you."

Roman stands up to grab a few clean napkins and some mini carrot cakes from the dessert table. He cleans in between my legs with one of the napkins, then feeds me a piece of cake. I'm ravenous and it's so delicious that I lick the corner of my mouth, getting every bit of the cream cheese frosting.

"Yummy."

"Are you cold, baby?" he asks.

"No, I'm perfect."

"Yes, you are."

I still blush whenever Roman pays me a compliment, and I probably always will because this man still gives me those first-day butterflies. The feeling you have when he kisses you for the first time or when he looks at you like there is no other woman in the world.

"Duchess, I almost forgot, what did you have to tell me?"

I immediately stop chewing my food. I don't know if I should tell him my secret or not. Maybe now's not the time when everything is so perfect.

"I didn't give you my wedding present," I say.

"Is that all?" He sounds relieved. "You know I wasn't expecting anything. I've got everything I could ever want or need in you and Knox."

We sit back on a different couch and Roman takes one of the throw blankets and wraps it around us as we sit back and reflect on the beautiful evening behind and ahead of us. We are pulling farther and farther away from the coastline and soon it will really just be us and the stars.

"I want to give it to you, anyway."

"Is it in your luggage? I can open it when we go to the suite later."

"No, it's in my handbag over there."

Roman grabs my bag and hands it to me. I pull out a long, rectangular box with a black satin bow around it and hand it to him.

"Hmm," he shakes it playfully. "I wonder what it is."

"Dunno." I shrug my shoulders.

I hold my breath as he opens the box. He stares

at it for a long moment, and I watch with some trepidation as his inky eyes become watery.

"What is this, Elizabeth?"

"You know what it is."

"You're pregnant?"

My gift is a positive pregnancy test sitting on a bed of white cotton stuffing.

"Congratulations, you've knocked me up again." I lie on top of him and kiss his chin. "I hope you're okay about this. I promise you I won't be as crazy and clingy as I was with the first one."

Romans quiets me with a kiss and lays a hand on my stomach.

"I am definitely okay with this, Duchess."

"Really?"

"You're going to be *soooo* fucking horny for nine months."

I slap his chest.

"You've got some serious problems in the head."

"Yeah, imagine how nuts our kids are going to be."

I burrow myself farther into his body.

"If they grow up to be anything like you, I'll be more than thrilled."

"Thank you for creating another extension of us, baby. I'm going to love you three so hard."

"You already do."

As we glide through the waves toward our future, I feel myself becoming even further enraptured by this man, and a tear falls from one of my eyes because I'm so stinking happy.

He pulls me into him and gently kisses my closed lids, savoring the taste of my tears. He kisses my mouth, and my body completely melts against his.

This is my husband.

The man who gives me all of the feels just like the night he grabbed my hand and helped me off the crowded dance floor.

The man who fights for me.

The man who adores me.

Our relationship may seem unusual to some, but this is what love looks like when it's Masterson made.

A love that was perfectly made just for me.

EPILOGUE

ELIZABETH

I check the clock for probably the fifth time in the last thirty minutes because Roman is late. I know that I may be behaving irrationally, but since the shooting I'm frequently nervous when he's late. I wonder if some other crazy person with a vendetta against me or my husband will strike.

I don't want to be that kind of wife, though. The neurotic one always checking up on her husband if he's five minutes late for dinner. So instead I call Sloan to pass the time away until he returns. If there's one person who's going to distract me from myself, it's my bestie.

"You getting ready to go?"

"Yeah, I just wanted to say hi before we leave in the morning," I tell a half-truth. "How are things?"

"So... you wanted to call me right before you leave for one of the most important trips of your life? I'm honored."

"It's not that big of a deal, Sloan. I've given these talks before."

"Wait, a minute. Did you just say that my best friend giving a Ted Talk on the main stage is not a big deal? You must still have baby brain, because I almost slept with my new boss so I could get the time off just to come see you wow the audience in Canada."

"You did not!?" I laugh hysterically. "He's way too old for you."

"I said almost, didn't I? Even for you, I couldn't bring myself to do it."

"You were never really coming with us to Canada, anyway."

"Not after the dark knight made it quite clear that this is a family trip and I wasn't welcomed."

"He never said that," I chuckle. "You always try to make him out to be a dark overlord when he's nothing of the kind."

"He's your husband. Of course you would think

his shit smells like roses. Hey, where are those scrumptious kiddies? The house sounds so quiet."

Surprisingly, I was not only pregnant on my wedding day, but I was pregnant with twins. Roman and I are now parents to two-year-old Knox and six-month-old twin boys, Seven and Bronx. I am seriously outnumbered in the house now.

"Mona is double checking the luggage. You know me. I'm afraid I might forget something. I swear I have squirrel brain lately since getting ready for this talk. I guess I'm a little more nervous than I thought I'd be."

"That's so cool that the president of Cabot nominated you for the talk. I bet his influence went a long way in you making the cut."

"Yeah, I have to say that it's been awesome working with him this past year."

"I guess it also doesn't hurt that he and Roman chat it up like they're old buddies now that he knows the prez has zero interest in you."

Turns out that the ring on Jacob's finger is because he's been lovingly married to his husband Bill for five wonderful years. He mentioned it in passing during one of our calls, and Roman's ears perked up like a busybody in church. He had the stupidest grin on his face for the rest of the night. It's kind of nutty but sweet how Roman thinks every single man on the planet would pursue me if given the chance.

"I can definitely admit that Jacob is hands-down my favorite client."

"And don't forget your most lucrative. School Bucks is being used by five universities thanks to him, not to mention that awesome write up you got in *US News and World Report*."

"That's true. Maybe I should name my next baby after him."

"There better not be a next baby," she laughs. "You two already have enough kids."

"Roman still wants that girl though."

"You two could afford to go to one of those places where they separate the X and Y chromosomes in a Petri dish and guarantee you the sex of the baby."

"We'd never do that. The whole fun is making the baby the old-fashioned way." I giggle.

"The luggage is all packed, Elizabeth."

Mona is our new full-time nanny and the daughter of one of Juliette's close friends. She's a quiet, studious girl who works for us while she studies general education at the local community college. She enters my office with one twin in her arms and Knox and Mr. Tibbs following right behind her. I think they're both smitten with her.

"Thanks, Mona."

"Seven is napping, but this one here can't seem to keep his eyes closed."

I stretch out my arms to hold Bronx. He is the more energetic of my twins and seems to function on very little sleep. Seven requires lots of naps and can be a bit more temperamental. Both of them look like mini versions of their father, and I can see parts of his personality in each.

These days my life is overflowing with dirty diapers, stuffed animals, story time and endless amounts of Cheerios but it's also bursting with rewarding work, laughs, occasional nights out with girlfriends and lots of passionate nights between me and Roman. We have blissfully found the balance in our relationship that once eluded us.

Knox grabs my leg and stares disapprovingly of us. He definitely has been more clingy since the boys were born. That's why I am making it a point to take all three of them with me on this trip to Canada. Where one goes, we all will go. That's our new family motto.

"Bitsy!"

I forgot that fast I was on the phone.

"Oops, sorry. I've got these two little stinkers clinging to me."

"Do you want me to take him?" Mona interrupts.

"No, I've got him. You can go study for a while until Seven wakes up. You have that major test on Friday, right?"

"Yes, I do and I'm pretty nervous about it."

"Okay go cram for an hour. I've got this."

I snicker as Knox and the dog follow right behind her like she's the pied piper.

"So let me get this straight," Sloan says. "You pay some pretty, young thing with the tightest ass I've ever seen an ungodly sum of money to watch your babies *and* to study?"

"We will not talk about this again. The only ass my husband wants is mine. He almost died trying to get back to it."

"Ooh-wee! Now that's what I like to hear. I'm drowning in the confidence that's dripping through this phone right now. All I was trying to say was, couldn't you have picked an older or uglier nanny? What do you think Roman is, some sort of saint?"

"Hardly, but what I do think is that my husband loves me and if I worried about every pretty young girl that crossed his path, we wouldn't be together at all. Between the club, the restaurant, and his other business ventures, he's around beautiful women all the time. If I trust him with my life, I can certainly trust him around other women."

"I guess I have trust issues."

"Yeah, and you're going to have to work on that before you meet the one."

"Girl, there is no *one* for me."

"I bet you've already met him."

"Unless you want me to marry the sweet old man that owns the dry cleaner's around the corner, I don't think I've met him."

I'm giggling at Sloan's comment when I hear the distinct tones of someone pressing the buttons of our digital front door lock. Finally, he's home.

"You're late."

"Hang the phone up and give me that mouth."

"Gotta go, Sloan."

"Yuck, I heard. Good luck tomorrow!"

Roman wraps one arm around my waist, kisses Bronx's forehead, and then goes in for a heated kiss.

"You look sexy today," he compliments.

"I'm in sweats."

"Yeah, but you're in your good sweats."

I laugh as he takes Bronx out of my arms and holds him in the air. The baby squeals with joy.

"The Kings wanted me to let you know how

proud they are of you. Getting a Ted Talk at your age is no easy feat. You're going to wow the audience with all your nerdy shit."

I slap Roman's shoulder by impulse forgetting that he's still sore there.

"Ouch, watch the merchandise," he warns playfully.

"Oops, sorry."

"The Kings bought us a bottle of Dom Pérignon to celebrate. I told them you were still breastfeeding the twins, but the Kings don't really do flowers."

"I can take a small sip. It won't kill the boys. That was sweet of them."

"They're just a bunch of softies when you get down to it."

"Uh, I wouldn't go that far."

"Where are my other two little monsters?"

"Knox is with Mona and Seven is sleeping. You should get your oldest though because I gave Mona a break to study. I'm sure he's bothering her."

"Let the boy have his crush."

"He's two-years-old."

"He gets it honestly."

"Can you believe he pulled a sunflower out of my vase and gave it to her the other day? The whole thing toppled over. Water was everywhere. I can't imagine where he got that from. Do Sesame Street characters give each other flowers?"

"I hope you got that on camera."

"Of course not. You know I always miss recording the best moments because I'm living them."

"So true, Duchess."

I lean over and initiate another kiss. This one is less rushed, but still full of passion. He gazes into my eyes with worship and longing, and I return the sentiment. For a moment, we almost forget that he's holding Bronx between us when I finally release his mouth.

"Damn," he comments.

That's exactly it in a nutshell. Our kisses still feel like they did the first time. When life feels like it's spinning out of control and the world is turning way too fast, a kiss from my husband is exactly what I need to stop, get off the rollercoaster and appreciate the view. Life is good, but life with Roman makes it spectacular.

Suddenly Knox runs into the room and grabs his father around the leg.

"Daddy!"

"Sorry guys, I didn't mean to interrupt, but Knox heard his dad's voice," Mona says.

"Hey, little monster. Were you helping Mona

pack for our big trip?" He rubs the top of Knox's massive head of hair.

"Yes!" He nods his head. "I helped."

"Awesome!"

"Is Seven still asleep, Mona?"

"Yes, I haven't heard a peep from him."

"Little dude needs his rest so his bones can grow," Roman says. "He's going to be the biggest one out of the three. I bet you."

Roman hands Bronx over to Mona. He lifts up Knox and tosses him up way too high in the air for my liking several times and then puts him back on the floor.

"Knox, why don't you and Bronx help Mona study. Mommy and I are going to finish our packing." Roman winks at me.

There was a time where I would have resisted this, been almost embarrassed by it, but this man is my husband and I will never take his love or his wanting me for granted again. I'm not a terrible mom because I want a little midday lovin' with my husband. What I am is a better wife and a happier human being.

Juliette tried to explain it to me when I wasn't ready to receive it, but I realize now that nothing in this life is promised. There's no guarantee that every time either of us leaves this house that we will both return. So living each day like it could be our last is the biggest gift of love we could ever give to our sons and to each other.

Mona heads off to study with Bronx in her arms and Knox skipping excitedly behind her. This time Mr. Tibbs stays right where he is underneath one of the kitchen chairs.

Roman holds out his massive hand towards me and I place mine inside of it.

"Shall we go finish packing?"

"Yes, I think we better."

He surprises me with a sudden whack on my butt.

"Then let's get going, Mrs. Masterson. I'm taking you on a long ride tonight and we don't make a stop until I fucking say so."

"Yes, Masterson."

SPINOFF SERIES ALERT!

Ready for your next alpha antihero? Get ready for the steamy spinoff series featuring Roman's best friends, The King Brothers. Read Jade & Camden

King's super HOT and twisted story in **CLAIMED**
first.

TAP TO DOWNLOAD THE BOOK INSTANTLY

AND GRAB THE SERIES ORIGIN STORY

Joseph Loves Juliette

How did Joseph and Juliette Masterson Fall In Love?

TAP TO DOWNLOAD THE BOOK INSTANTLY

LISA LANG BLAKENEY

Want to peek in at our favorite couple several years later when Knox is a teen?
As a special gift, I will be sending my VIP newsletter subscribers this bonus epilogue very soon. Make sure you're on the list!
SUBSCRIBE HERE

Note From Lisa

Thank you for taking time out of your busy life to read another installment of Roman and Elizabeth's love story. This novel wasn't in my release schedule this year but Roman would not be silenced. Lol! (He's a chatty one.)

I want to thank the wonderful readers in my Romance Ninja readers group for helping me name Roman and Elizabeth's son, Knox. I'm so grateful that I have a group of wonderful readers and friends in there. If you are new to me, please feel free to join us to chat and be notified of my upcoming releases and sales: http://lisalangblakeney.com/community

Stay Safe,
Lisa

WHERE YOU CAN FIND ME

MY VIP LIST (Get the nitty gritty)

I have a VIP Reader mailing list. I only send free books, new release, sales or special giveaway information to this group. No spam. You can join here: http://LisaLangBlakeney.com/VIP .

MY PRIVATE FAN GROUP (Casual fun)

Join my private Fan Group on Facebook also known as my "Romance Ninja Warriors" where I share all things new going on, celebrate birthdays, post teasers, yummy pics, giveaways and just chit chat. http://LisaLangBlakeney.com/community

MY ARC TEAM (Review my books)

I have a special ARC team. If you enjoy my books

and would like a free advanced reader copy of my next book in exchange for an honest review on release day, then feel free to apply. There are only a certain number of slots with each release and participation is strictly enforced, but I'd love to have you:) To apply, please go here: http://lisalangblakeney.com/arc-reviewers/

LISA LANG
BLAKENEY

Joseph Loves Juliette

How did Joseph and Juliette Masterson Fall In Love?

Whatever she wants.

Whenever she wants it.

However she likes it.

As teenagers, it was love at first sight for Joseph Masterson and Juliette Hill, but they were from completely different worlds and it wasn't meant to be. When the two have a second chance meeting as adults, they discover that the powerful chemistry between them is still there and stronger than ever. But this time there's no way he's letting her go. In fact, this time, his mission is to give Juliette the world or die trying.

READ NOW
Book #5 Masterson Series
Ebook or Print

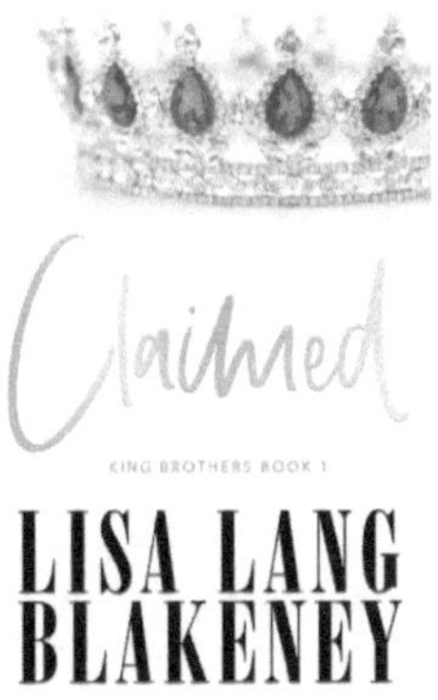

CLAIMED

Standalone Romance

Meet Alpha Camden King

I work for him, but I can't stand him. I slept with him once, and he never lets me forget it. Camden King thinks he can have me again...and again...and again. But he can't...I won't let that happen. I just have to last thirty days to prove it to him. Will I be able to hold out? Or have I finally met my match...

READ NOW

AVAILABLE ON AUDIO

Add To Goodreads

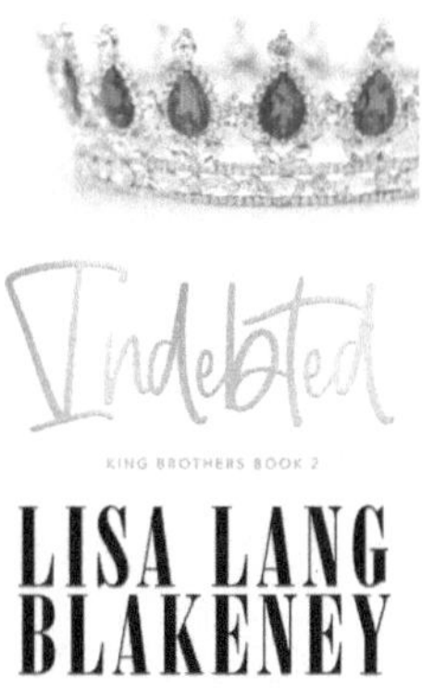

INDEBTED

Standalone Romance

Meet Alpha Cutter King

There's something about Cutter King that reminds me of every bad relationship I've been in and every bad decision I've ever made...

READ NOW

AVAILABLE ON AUDIO NOW!

Add To Goodreads

LISA LANG BLAKENEY

BROKEN
Standalone Romance

Meet Alpha Stone Barringer
First he lied to me.
Then he seduced me.
Now he's broken me.

READ NOW
AVAILABLE ON AUDIO
Add To Goodreads

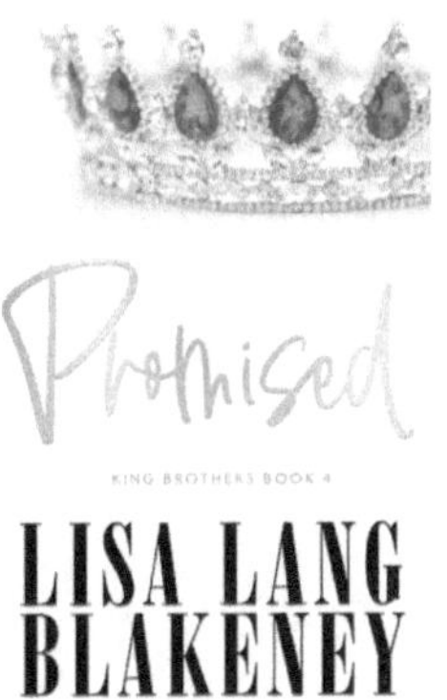

PROMISED

King Brother Drama.

King Brother Hotness.

A King Happily Ever After.

Novella Length

You are cordially invited to A King Family Wedding.
The question is which one of the Kings will make it
to the altar?

READ NOW

AVAILABLE ON AUDIO

Coming Soon. Get Notified!

ABOUT THE AUTHOR

Lisa Lang Blakeney is an international bestselling author of contemporary romance sold in more than 28 countries. Worried that her fellow PTO moms might disapprove, she wrote and published her steamy debut novel Masterson under a different title and pen name in August of 2015.

Thanks to strong reader support of her alpha male character, Roman Masterson, she was encouraged to continue with the series and published the entire Masterson Trilogy the following year. She hasn't looked back since and continues to write novels featuring strong alpha men and the smart women they seek to claim.

A romance junkie for sure, you can find Lisa watching a romantic comedy, reading a romance novel, or writing one of her own most days of the week. If she's not doing that, she's outside in the garden tending to her roses.

Lisa is the wife of one alpha (whom she met in college), mother to four girls, and two labradoodles. Get news on releases, sales and giveaways when you become one of Lisa's VIP readers at : http://LisaLangBlakeney.com/VIP

www.ingramcontent.com/pod-product-compliance
Lightning Source LLC
Chambersburg PA
CBHW061519210726
48287CB00006B/1742